THE SNOW SINGER

by

Florine De Veer

ISBN-13:9781492117384

DEDICATION

To my family members who were children when this book was first written
and to their children and their grandchildren in hopes that no matter what age
they are they will still enjoy it.

ACKNOWLEDGMENT

Warm thanks to David A. Phelps for the cover art

CONTENTS

Prologue: by Rowan

The princess was born in the golden autumn, when the trees were rich with hues of crimson and bronze, hanging heavy with nuts and apples, and the fields were laden for harvest. I had been busy in the forest since dawn with duties concerning bird and beast, tree and flower, and I was not particularly on the lookout for the royal sign that day. But when I returned to my cottage and found Madoc the Forester there, I knew at once why he had come.

"Great news, Rowan!" he called out as I stepped across the threshold. "A princess has been born this afternoon!"

I clapped my hands and murmured thanks to the One Who Hears.

"It was a long birthing," he continued," but the babe is well and strong, they say."

"And Varena?" I asked. "How is she?"

"Queen Varena is tired but filled with joy. She is asking for you. Will you go to her?"

"Yes, of course," I said, and reached for the cloak I had just hung up.

"King Verl is delighted. He has forgotten he ever wished for a son, and is acting as if he invented babies!" Madoc added, and both of us laughed. That was the nature of our warmhearted king. He was an impulsive, loving man.

"There will be feasting and merrymaking in the village as well as the castle tonight," I said. "Will you walk back with me, Madoc? Or you are welcome to rest awhile in my cottage."

"I will rest, and then I must go home and share the good news with my old mother. She has been waiting for this."

Yes, many people had been waiting. King Verl and Queen Varena were dear to their people. And Varena was dearer to me than anyone on earth. I had cared for her when she was a child, and taught her as she grew. I alone had known, for I have many gifts, that the pretty little blacksmith's daughter, running around the village with bare feet, would one day be Queen, and I had seen to it that she learned things needful for such a destiny.

As I walked swiftly through the gathering twilight I thought back on the day that the king had first seen her, dancing with the other village maidens around the maypole. It had not been I who had brought him there, though I knew that people thought so. It was fated that he would eventually meet and love her. And love her he did, at first sight – and who could blame him, for she was as beautiful as the spring morning in which she danced.

Yes, he loved her, and she him, and their love and gladness overcame the objections of many people who felt that a king should marry someone of royal blood. Even the queen mother gave in at last, and the High King himself sent a wedding gift.

How happy King Verl's mother would have been had she lived to see this day! She had longed so for grandchildren.

Swiftly as I walked, it was full night before I emerged from the woods behind the royal palace. The towers rising above the stone walls were gemmed with golden light from every window, and colored fire shot up in showers from the great tower, where fireworks were being lighted in honor of the royal birth. The guards must be within their guardhouse, celebrating with wine, for no one challenged me as I approached. The kingdom of Verlain had been so long at peace that the guards were ever made overly comfortable, but usually there was one, at least, on the wall. I did not disturb them, but wrapped myself in shadow and let the night breeze lift me over the wall. As shadow I entered the castle and drifted up the winding staircase to the queen's chambers. Not until I reached her boudoir did I take my own form.

She lay in the great bed, her golden hair spread around her, as bright as the threads of the canopy over the bedstead. The cradle stood a few feet away but neither maid nor nurse was to be seen.

"I sent them away," she said, her sleepy blue eyes glowing up at me. "I knew you would come, and I wanted to see you alone.

3

I made them bring the cradle in here so that I could have my darling near me. Look at her, Rowan. Is she not the fairest babe in the world?"

I bent obediently over the cradle, and I could in all honesty say that she was. Most newborn infants are red and wrinkled, but the new princess had skin as clear and white as milk. Her bits of hair curled already in jet black ringlets and her mouth was a rosebud.

"As soon as I saw her I remembered that silly wish I made," said Varena. "It *was* silly; I knew that when I said it, but perhaps mothers are always a bit silly. Thank you, Rowan."

I smiled down at her. I did not ask why she was thanking me. We both knew that I had done what I could to fulfill her fond, foolish, innocent wish. It had been on the occasion of a snowfall – a rare happening in the Southern Kingdoms – and the queen had been sitting by the window at her ebony embroidery frame. She had pricked her finger, and a drop of blood had fallen on the snow edging the window.

"Oh, do not worry," she had said as her maid hurriedly brought a handkerchief to bind the wounded finger. "It is nothing. How lovely the red looks against the snow," she had added dreamily. "If I could have a wish, I would have a little girl with skin as white as snow, lips as red as blood, and hair as black as this frame."

The eldest of the maid of honor had replied, "A first child should always be a boy, an heir for the kingdom."

But I had touched Varena's hand and given her a smile that told her I sympathized with her wish. For a prince belongs to his father, but a daughter is company and joy to her mother, even one of royal blood.

"Verl is just as pleased as if she had been a boy," Varena added. "He says she has his mother's eyes."

"And she does."

"And – and we are young, I told him. We will have a son, many sons perhaps." There was a slight catch to her voice. "He said not to think of that now, only to enjoy our daughter."

That was generous of him. He must have seen how very tired she was. Indeed, knowing the king, I guessed he had spent the whole time of the birthing pacing the corridor, suffering agony of mind. He must have been exhausted himself.

Varena's eyes had fluttered shut as I lowered the babe back into the cradle and moved to her side. She was breathing slowly, and in the moonlight she looked as white as marble. I touched her hand. Her eyes opened and she smiled.

"Rowan – dearest friend – I am so tired... It is hard to think of days to come but – I wanted to – to ask you..."

I leaned over her and my own words came through a thickness in my throat. "Ask me whatever you wish, my darling."

"My child – if – if aught should happen to me – You will be a friend to her, will you not?"

"I shall be a friend to her no matter what befalls."

"And – teach her and – protect her? A princess needs powerful friends."

"I shall be her godmother," I promised. "She will, of course, have noble godparents appointed to her, and friends in high places. But as a token of my promise I now give her the name by which she will be known. I call her Neva, the white one, and I will be near her always."

"Neva. What a lovely name." The queen smiled and a look of deep peace came over her face. "Thank you, Rowan. Now I can sleep."

As her eyes closed again I bent and kissed her cold cheek. I drew the coverlet up under her chin, and then I walked to the window and stood gazing out into the blazing night sky.

I was born with many gifts and powers. I have the ability to see what will be, to weave and manipulate certain threads of fate, to move them in other directions. But I cannot really change what must be, and I am helpless to prolong the life of any being. The moment I had touched Varena's hand I had felt the darkness that had already brushed her. My heart was heavy with the bitter knowledge. She might have a day or even a week in which to take

6

joy in her daughter. But Queen Varena would never again leave her royal bedroom until they carried her out to her last rest.

Chapter One
The Gift

On the morning of her twelfth birthday Princess Neva woke very early. The heavy silk that covered her windows had not yet been opened and the room was dim, but she knew somehow that the sun was just up. She sat up, listening, but there was no sound from the antechamber, where her maids slept. She was glad to have some time to herself, for the day would be a busy one. She was going to have a party, and among the guests was Liam, son of Kervyn, the High King. The whole palace was excited over it. It was the first time he had visited Verlain since he was a small boy and everyone said it was a great honor.

Neva wasn't sure whether she should be nervous about having such an important guest or not, but she liked what she had seen of the prince when they had met in the Great Hall last night. He was quite handsome, and his smile was friendly. He had not looked half as arrogant as, say, Eris of Vichille, who, though only Neva's age, wore a proud and haughty air.

Neva wished her father could be here at the party, but unfortunately the giants of the Western Wildlands had chosen to attack the borders of Verlain only a week ago, and he had ridden off with his army to deal with them. It had been too late to call off Neva's birthday party, for many of the guests were already on their way. So she was left to represent the kingdom on her own, which was a great responsibility but rather exciting. If only she could be sure her father would be all right, she would be, she thought, perfectly happy.

She slipped out of the great bedstead and crossed the thickly woven carpet to the window. Pulling the silks aside she climbed up on the window seat and pushed the window open. The scent of roses came up from the garden below, and a cool breeze brushed her face. Pale gold sunshine was just emerging from a curtain of grey and pink dawn. Down in the village a rooster crowed and a dog barked. Soon the castle gates would open for the tradesmen who brought their goods to the king's house, and the day would start, but now it was very still. She could slip out to the garden and back before she was missed.

She dressed quickly in a plain gown, leaving her hair loose on her shoulders, and stole softly through the adjoining chamber, where Linet and Silvi, her two favorite attendants, slept. They did not stir. The bed where her old nurse Aga used to sleep was empty.

Now that Neva was twelve she no longer needed a nurse, only maids of honor. She would miss Aga, but it was nice to be growing up. And it would be easier to get away with things like slipping out to the garden at dawn without being caught. Aga used to always wake up, as if she had an extra sense to tell her when the princess was about to do something improper.

Neva stepped cautiously into the corridor, but no one was around yet. Opposite the door to her chambers was a thick tapestry, which hid another door, a small one that opened onto a flight of stone steps. No one knew about this door except Neva and her godmother Rowan. Neva often wondered whether it was hidden to other eyes by some magic. The steps led straight down to another door, which opened directly into the garden.

The early morning fragrance of roses met her as she ran lightly down the path to the little square bower that she loved most of all. And Rowan was there, as Neva had known she would be.

"May joy be with you this memory day of your birth, little one," said Rowan.

"Oh, I am glad you have come!" Neva said, hugging her. "Prince Liam is here, Rowan, did you know? I was not nervous about receiving all the guests alone until he arrived. It is a great honor."

"Yes, but you need not be nervous over it. Others are more aware of the honor than is the prince himself. He is like his father, free from arrogance in every way. I think you will like him."

"Yes, I thought so when I first saw him," Neva agreed. "He has a pleasant smile. But you will come to the feast, won't you? I will be so much more comfortable if you are there."

"I cannot come, my child," said Rowan. "I must set off on a journey today."

Neva was surprised. She had never known Rowan to go away, at least not any further than to a neighboring village or sometimes to gather herbs in the mountains. Those were not journeys, only small excursions.

"Why, where are you going?" she asked.

"To the east border, where the battle is. Your father needs me more than you do right now."

A cold hand seemed to touch Neva's heart. She loved her father more than anyone in the world. "The battle..." she began unsteadily.

"The battle is over and the giants were defeated. But he was slightly wounded and is resting in the palace of Princess Melyni, and I should be with him."

"Only slightly wounded?"

"I promise. He is not in danger of death."

"Then why are you going?"

"I cannot explain it all to you now. You will understand someday. You must trust me that I would not go on your birthday, like this, if it were not necessary."

"Of course I trust you," said Neva, and she did. There were many things Rowan could not, or would not, explain to her; it had always been so. Neva had the greatest respect for her godmother's special gifts and tried not to ask questions. But it was hard when it concerned her father.

"Who is Princess Melyni?" she asked after a silence.

"She rules the East Kingdom of Prayn. Have you not learned of the witch queens of Prayn? The last was her mother, Kilse, who died in the same year you were born. Melyni has renounced the heritage of witchcraft and sworn fealty to the High King. To show the world that she is in earnest, she will not even call herself Queen, but keeps the title of Princess."

Neva remembered learning a little about the defeat of the Witch-Queen Kilse in her history lessons, but very little. It had been hinted that Rowan herself could tell the true story best. She wondered if that was so, but did not ask. If Rowan wanted her to know the story she would have told her.

Rowan nodded and said, as if reading her thoughts, "It is a long and dark history, but perhaps you are old enough to hear it now. When I come back I will tell it to you. Now, before I go, I have a gift for you. Come with me."

They walked through the garden to a small cottage at the far end. This was Rowan's place at the palace, where she could almost always be found if Neva needed her. Her real home, Neva knew, was somewhere in the forest but, especially when Neva was young, Rowan had usually stayed at her palace home. It was a cozy little place and Neva had often spent an afternoon or evening there, learning things not usually taught to princesses, such as how to sweep a floor, cleanse a pot, or brew a healing potion.

As they entered the small kitchen her eyes were drawn to the table, where sat a tiny basket made of woven rushes. It was just such a basket as many of the village women made, but Neva had never seen one so small, or gilded with silver and gold as this one was. It almost seemed to shine in its own light. It had a smooth, gleaming cover.

"It looks faerie made," she said.

"Better than that," said Rowan. "It is dwarf made. Deep in the heart of the forest live Redstol the dwarf and his sons. They mine the mountains for silver and gold, as dwarves usually do, but his second youngest son Thunel has other gifts. He weaves baskets, tends a garden, makes wreaths and bridal bouquets and the like. He even makes lace."

13

Neva was amazed. She had never heard of a dwarf like that.

"Some scorn him, and the dwarf king will not admit him to the Metal Circle, which all grown dwarves join in their one hundredth year – that is when they reach maturity. But Redstol feels that Thunel's gifts are valid ones, and that each individual has the right to walk the path natural to him. He allows Thunel to do what he does best."

"And Thunel made this?" Neva asked, touching the basket gently.

"I asked him to make it for you. Open it."

The lid fell back on silver hinges. Inside lay a plain black key and an even plainer blue stone. Nothing more. Neva couldn't help feeling disappointed but she didn't say anything. Rowan laughed softly.

"They do not look like much, do they? And I cannot even tell you what they truly are, you must discover that for yourself."

"Are they – magic?" Neva asked with new interest.

"They are things of power. The stone was left with me to give to you on your twelfth birthday. I was not told what it would do."

"Left with you? By whom?" This was surprising.

"By the Lady of the People. She is my godmother, as I am yours, and Queen of the Good Folk. Few see her in these times. I

14

myself have only seen her twice. She came to me on the day your mother and father were wed and said these words: *A daughter will be born of the royal house of Verlain. At the start of her twelfth year give her the stone to carry with her always.*"

Neva was breathless. A gift from the Queen of the Faerie! It had been centuries and more since any of the Faerie – save those like Rowan with some of the old blood in them – had concerned themselves with humankind. Everyone said that, even her tutor, who was not convinced that such beings even existed. Why now? And what was it?

She lifted it out of the basket rather nervously. It was no bigger than a pebble, smooth and dull blue. It felt weightless in her hand. A tiny loop had been attached to it, so that she could hang it from a cord or a wrist band.

"I will wear it always," she said.

"The key is from me. It will open doors for you if ever you need any opened. I can say no more than that."

"I will keep it with me always, too," said Neva, but she was uneasy. Always her gifts from Rowan had been unusual but fun, and without mystery. Harps with golden strings, carved birds that really sang, balls that came back to the owner when called. Of course, Neva thought, she had been younger, then. She was

15

twelve now. No longer a child. Why in another four years she might be married!

Rowan put on a thick cloak and took up her wooden walking stick. Neva hooked her tiny basket over her wrist and they left the cottage.

"Give my love to my father, and tell him I pray that he will soon return," said the princess.

"I will. Now run in before your maids wake up and miss you. May you have a happy day, my darling," said Rowan and kissed her.

Neva ran across the garden to the postern. There she turned to look back. Although there was no gate in the wall and no way out except this door, she was not surprised to find herself alone. Rowan was gone.

Chapter Two
The Snow Bird

As Neva fumbled with the doorknob she heard a whistle above her. It didn't sound like any bird she knew, so she looked up. There was a balcony with a crenellated wall around it overlooking the garden. It opened off a portrait gallery, which ran not far from the guest apartments kept for the High King, should he or any of his family visit. And looking over the balcony, smiling down at her was the prince himself.

"Merry Name Day, Princess Neva!" he called. "May I come down and join you? Your garden is beautiful."

Neva was quite sure that her maids and the prince's attendants and everyone else would be shocked. Royal personages were never supposed to be on their own, unattended. On the other hand, how could she say no to the son of the High King?

She dropped a hasty curtsey and called back, "Of course you are welcome here, Your Highness. But the only way to get down is through my apartments and I think – that is, I am afraid my maids..."

"Yes, my gentlemen, too. They are always officious and I am forever shocking them. But I think I can climb down. I have had a good deal of practice in climbing."

He swung himself over the wall. Neva gasped, sure he would fall and break his neck, but he did not. He found hand and foot holds invisible from below, and moments later he was standing beside her, grinning.

"Did I not tell you?" he asked, his eyes sparkling. "I climb out of my bedroom window and go down to the shore very often, before anyone awakes to stop me. I am the despair of all my attendants and my royal mother. My father only laughs. I think he did the same when he was young."

Neva found herself grinning back. It was impossible not to.

"I slip out here often," she confessed. "It is my own garden, which my godmother Rowan made for me. Linet and Silvi, my maids, are dears but they *fuss* so! I like to come alone."

"Oh, I know!" He pulled a stern face and mimicked a coldly polite manner. "*Your Highness! You will tear your doublet! A prince does not clamber over the rocks! A prince does not go off on his own! A prince does not enjoy himself!*"

Neva giggled. "Do they really say that – that you aren't supposed to enjoy yourself?"

"Well, not in so many words. But that is certainly what they mean! But let us not worry about them. I want to get acquainted with you. I have heard so much about you."

"About me?"

"Certainly. I hear about all the rulers of the kingdoms and their families, but I have been especially interested in you because they say you have a faerie godmother. Is it true?"

"Rowan has faerie blood, but she is not a faerie," Neva said. "She has gifts, but she never talks about them, and I have never asked many questions. If you had come out five minutes ago you would have met her."

"I would like to meet her. My father knows her and speaks highly of her."

Neva was pleased about that. She liked Rowan to be appreciated.

"She is on her way to the Kingdom of Prayn on the Eastern Border. My father defeated the giants but he was wounded and is recovering in the royal palace there. Rowan says he was not badly wounded, but she feels as if he needs her."

Prince Liam frowned slightly. He said, "Princess Melyni rules Prayn."

"Yes, that is what Rowan said."

"I have not met her but –" he hesitated – "she comes of the line of the Witch Queens."

"But hasn't she sworn allegiance to your father? Rowan said she had."

"Yes she has," said Liam, "and I have no right to hold her heritage against her. I have never seen her, only heard talk of her."on a low-hanging branch of a nearby tree, and Neva sat on a bench across from him. The sun was up, now, spilling light the color of honey across the garden. It turned the prince's pale hair to gold and glistened on the embroidery of his collar. It turned the dewdrops on the grass into glittering diamonds. It was going to be a beautiful day.

19

"Can we have your birthday ball out here in the garden?" asked the prince.

"If you command it, we can, Your Highness," said Neva.

"Do call me Liam. I think we will be friends. And why not if you command it? It is your home and your birthday."

"I don't think Mother Desma, who is in charge of the ceremony, would listen to a command from me. She hasn't realized that I'm growing up," said Neva. "Even though my father left me to represent the kingdom in his absence, everyone from my maids of honor to the men at arms still considers me a mere baby."

"My mother still does not really believe that I am growing up, either," said Liam. "Nor do most of *my* attendants. I quite understand what you mean."

"But you are a boy, and the Crown Prince, so it can't be as bad as it is for me," Neva said.

"Perhaps not. Especially since I had my fourteenth birthday and was made a knight."

"A knight! At fourteen!" Neva was impressed.

"It's only a title, of course. It isn't as if I have fought dragons or delivered castles or done anything else to earn knighthood. I felt almost embarrassed when Sir Loris, who has fought in dozens of battles, presented me with my white belt."

"You will earn it someday," Neva said.

"Yes, I hope so. I would like to go adventuring all alone, like the knights of King Arthur did."

"So would I! But of course princesses only have adventures if they are carried off by giants or dragons or other nasty creatures, and that doesn't sound like much fun. And then they have to wait and hope some adventuring knight will come and deliver them."

"That is so. It doesn't seem fair, does it? All maidens should be allowed to learn how to handle a sword, just in case."

Neva wasn't sure whether he was laughing at her or not.

"No, really," he said, "or if not a sword, a dagger, for self defense. Not that a dagger would be much good against a dragon or giant – not unless you were very, very lucky."

"I've learned archery," Neva told him. "But from all I hear, arrows aren't much good against dragons, either. I think I will concentrate on not being carried off by anyone."

He burst into laughter. "A wise plan! But how did you happen to learn archery?"

"Oh, Rowan allowed Madoc, a forester who knows her quite well, to teach me. He says I am not too bad at it. But please don't tell – I am sure my father would be shocked."

"It is a secret between us," he promised. "And I will now tell you a secret, so we shall be even. I know how to embroider with silks. Of course it is not considered a manly thing to do, much less princely, but I always admired the pictures my mother and her ladies could create with their needles. And once, when I was only eight, I had a lung infection and was a long time getting well. And to amuse me, my old nurse taught me how."

"I will never tell," said Neva. She was flattered that he had entrusted her with such a secret.

"I wonder," she said, "who decided what arts were fit only for ladies and what were fit only for men? When you think of it, why should it be less manly to embroider than to paint portraits – and

21

many men do that. And why should ladies not be taught defensive arts?"

"I often think the world would be a happier place if folks stopped telling other folks what is right and proper," Liam agreed.

"Like the dwarf Thunel. He made my basket." She held it up to him and told him what she had learned about the maker.

"If I could create a thing like this, I wouldn't care whether or not I was allowed into a circle of miners," said the prince, examining it. "Look, he has woven little figures of birds and plants right into it. Such skill! I would like to meet this dwarf someday. I am greatly interested in craftsmen."

"Do you know any dwarves?" she asked. "I have never seen one."

"The chief swordsmith at home is a dwarf. He is the only one I know. They hardly ever leave the mountains. He makes other things besides swords – my mother's harp, for instance. A fine thing, with a sweeter tone than any I've ever heard. Also the doors to my father's throne room. They are of pure silver. You must come see them someday."

"I would like that! I've heard that the High King's palace is beautiful."

"It is very large and has fine things in it. But what I like best is that it is near the sea. In the evenings you can hear the singing of the merfolk, shrill and sweet and entrancing. You have to be careful not to listen too closely, of course, or you might be enchanted and throw yourself into the sea. But listening from a distance is perfectly safe, and delight enough. My mother has written down some of their songs."

"My voice teacher once told me that mer songs could not be translated into our music," said Neva, very impressed.

"Mer songs can be learned but they are very difficult. My mother's great grandmother was of the merfolk, and Mother is a talented musician. She told me to be sure to have you sing while I am here, for we have heard much about the beauty of your voice, and Mother is always interested in singers. A traveling bard told us, once, that your people call you the snow singer among themselves, because you sing like the mythical snow lark. I always wondered, though – why snow singer? It cannot often snow here."

""Oh," said Neva, blushing a little, "it is a silly story my maid Linet tells – how my mother wished once for a daughter as white as snow, as black as ebony, and as red as blood, and Rowan granted her the wish. Only a story. And my use-name Neva means white, of course. So I am called the snow singer among the people – or so they say. No one ever calls me that directly."

"Will you sing tonight? I would like to hear you."

Neva loved to sing and had no false modesty. She knew she had a lovely voice. She promised readily.

The sun was fully up by now, and through the open windows of the castle they could hear an unusual commotion.

"I think you have been missed," said Liam.

"More likely you have been missed. But we should go inside; it must be nearly time for breakfast. How will you get back?" She looked up at the balcony.

"The way I came, of course. To one used to climbing cliffs this wall is a mere trifle. Watch me!"

It seemed to be. He was up in a matter of moments. Still, Neva did not breathe until she saw him scramble over the balustrade.

"You see?" He leaned over, laughing. "No problem at all. Until we meet again, Princess Neva..."

Chapter Three
The Mirror

The party was held in the gardens, by Prince Liam's request, and was far more fun than the originally planned formal function would have been. That was also due to the prince. He had a way of making everyone relax and forget about who was of a higher rank than whom, or what was and was not proper. Instead of sitting stiffly in a row on a dais, while acrobats and other entertainers performed for them, he had them play games, sing and dance. Since the noble guests ranged from little Prince Gered of the tiny island kingdom of Lett, who was only six, to Lady Anaina of Elis, who was fifteen, getting them all to enjoy the evening was something of a feat. It took charm and tact and wit, all of which the young prince possessed in abundance.

"He is like his father," she overheard Anaina saying to Countess Daril, who was also fifteen. "Everyone loves the High King because he makes people comfortable. Prince Liam is the same. He will make a good king someday."

Neva did not sing until the evening was almost over, but once she began, no one wanted to do anything else but listen to her. She was pleased and excited, for she had not had many opportunities to sing before an audience. As her sweet, clear voice filled the garden the guests listened spellbound.

"I have never heard anything so lovely," said Countess Daril. "Not even the Princess Melyni of Prayn sings as beautifully, though she is so famous for her singing."

The party ended with a feast and gift giving. From Prince Liam, Neva received a sheaf of songs, bound in leather. When she looked through them she found songs from all around the world, and songs even of other peoples. There were dwarf songs, elf ballads, and even songs of the merfolk. It was a rare treasure.

"My mother put it together," he told her. "She says you must come to visit someday and sing some of them for us."

"I will," said Neva. "Someday when I am older and have learned them all."

It was a lovely party.

The next morning the guests began to depart. Because there had been a separate formal banquet for the parents and guardians of the young guests the night before, Neva had seen little of them. It was her duty now, however, to sit in her father's throne room as each group came to bid her farewell. It was a tedious business, especially since the prince and his escort had gone first. There was no one to ease the formality. She wondered when she would see him again, and if he would sometimes think of her.

The Countess Daril and her aunt were the last to leave. While they were saying goodbye, Mother Desma was distracted by a question from the aunt, and Neva seized the opportunity to ask Daril a private question.

"Last night you mentioned Princess Melyni," she said as they chatted a little more informally. "Have you met her?"

"Yes, at the High Court, when she came to swear fealty to the king. I was there. And once we stopped at the Castle of Prayn on our way to our country house. She is very beautiful. But they say she is proud, and cannot bear to hear of anyone more beautiful. She has a magic mirror, in which there is a captive truth-teller, who tells her every day that she is the fairest in the world – or at least so they say."

"Do you think that's true?" Neva asked, shocked.

"I think it is. Her mother had the power to enslave different spirits of air and water and fire. They say the mirror was a gift from her to her daughter. It *does* sound rather dreadful, doesn't it?" she added, as if thinking it over for the first time. "To entrap a powerful being and use it for something so – so trivial. If she made it work for the good of her kingdom it wouldn't be quite so bad."

It would be bad enough, thought Neva. Rowan had given her a deep respect for creatures born with natural powers. The idea of any of them being enslaved and forced to do any sort of magic was appalling. She wondered if Rowan knew about Princess Melyni's mirror.

After the countess and her escort had gone, Neva's day went back to its normal routine. She ate breakfast in her room, and then went to the learning hall, where her tutor, Master Piers, was waiting. She knew that many people thought book learning a waste of time for a princess, and had been shocked when the king engaged a tutor for her. A governess to teach her dance and music and etiquette would have been acceptable, but what did a girl, even a princess, need to know of history, languages, and such? But

Neva liked studying, and usually concentrated her whole mind on the day's lesson. Today, however, her thoughts kept wandering.

"Master Piers," she said suddenly, looking up from her grammar book, "when you taught me the history of the kingdoms, you didn't say much about the Kingdom of Prayn."

"We do not study history until tomorrow," said the tutor. "Pray concentrate on the lesson at hand, Princess."

There was no use in arguing with him. He was very strict. But a few hours later there was an interruption. A message had arrived for Neva from her father. This was important enough that the tutor could not override it.

The messenger was tall and thin, and wore a silver leopard stitched to his tunic. He had a rather arrogant manner, unusual with messengers, but when Neva thanked him for the message and told him that food and wine would be served to him immediately, he bowed and looked more pleasant.

"And why would a messenger of Prayn be bringing you a message from the king?" asked Master Piers in a troubled voice.

"He was wounded, and Princess Melyni took him in to care for him," said Neva, glancing over the message, which was no more than what Rowan had told her already. He said that she must not worry, that he was healing well. He did not say anything about Rowan being there, however, and that seemed odd. Surely she was there by now. She could travel like the wind when necessary.

She read the letter aloud to the tutor, partly because she knew he would want to hear it — he had taught the king when he was a boy, and loved him dearly — partly to show off her scholarship (it was written in the formal language known as Vernish), and partly to explain to him her interest in Prayn.

"Rowan told me yesterday that he was there," she added when she had finished. "I know Princess Melyni is descended from the Witch Queens of Prayn, but that she has sworn allegiance to the High King. But I would like to know more about her."

"She is very beautiful," said the tutor.

Neva was surprised. Master Piers did not normally bother with such superficial things as someone's appearance.

"I keep hearing that," she said. "And she sings beautifully, and she is rather proud."

"Of that I cannot say. She was here with her mother many years ago, when your father was a young man. Before he met your mother. There was talk, then, of an alliance of marriage between your father and Princess Melyni, but your grandmother, the queen, was reluctant to agree, and put it off. And when your father fell in love with your mother, the queen allowed him to marry for love instead of state."

Neva knew about her mother being a village girl. Rowan had told her the whole story when she was very small. And she knew her parents had married for love, and that some had been shocked, but that everyone had eventually accepted the young queen. But this was the first time she had heard that her mother had a rival.

"But he was not actually betrothed to Princess Melyni, was he?"

"Oh no. It had never gone so far. Still the dark queen – Melyni's mother – was not pleased. What the princess herself felt,

29

no one knows. Later, after her mother died, she sent a gift to your mother, and a message of goodwill. They say she is anxious to be accepted among the kingdoms, and to be rid of the name of witch. She has done nothing to darken her reputation over the years, save that she continues to live in the Castle of Prayn, which was built by witchcraft and has many – what shall I call them? – unpleasant instruments of magic in it – if one is to believe the minstrel's tales, which I myself seldom do," he added hastily.

Neva decided to give Princess Melyni the benefit of the doubt. Perhaps she did have a magic mirror, and that was pretty awful, but growing up with things of dark magic, perhaps she had never stopped to think how awful it was. And she was trying not to be a witch, everyone agreed about that. And she was caring for the king, and that was good.

"She can't help her mother or her home," she said, opening her books again. "I shall send her a message, thanking her for taking my father in. It was kind of her."

"Yes," said Master Piers but he sounded uncertain.

Neva sent the message to Princess Melyni, along with one to her father, telling him she longed for his recovery, and sending her love. Then she put the matter out of her mind as best she could. She went back to the routine of her days, studying and sewing and music, but she missed Rowan and wondered why she did not hear from her.

It was two months before the king finally returned home to Verlain. Overjoyed though she was to see him, Neva was shocked at how thin and pale he was. His wounds must have been worse than he had let on. He was indeed still so weak that as soon as he arrived he had to go to bed and rest from the journey. But the next day he sent for her to have breakfast with him, and he seemed himself again.

He told her about the battle, and how when the giants were defeated he had lost consciousness from his wounds, and had only awakened to find himself at Prayn. How the princess herself, who had great skill at healing, had looked after him, and seen that he had the best of everything. How his uneasiness at being in the Dark Castle soon wore off because of her kindness, and how grateful he was to her for her care. Then he asked about Neva's birthday party, and about all her activities since then, so it was much later, and breakfast was over, before she had a chance to ask about Rowan.

The king seemed surprised. "She was there for only a few hours," he said. "She came to see that I was being well cared for, and then she left. Are you sure she did not return to her own house in the woods?"

"I do not know," Neva said. "I never thought of that. But it isn't like her to come back and not visit me."

King Verl patted her hand. "I know she loves you, my child, but she often has other demands on her time. Do not worry, she will turn up when she has a spare moment."

Of course it was true that Rowan was friend and helper to many other people. Still, Neva was uneasy. That night before she went to bed she got out the gifts Rowan had given her. She had threaded a thin silver chain through the loop of the blue stone, and she wore it always as a pendant, but she had not looked at the basket and the key since her birthday. She was surprised to find

31

that the key was not black, as she remembered it, but more of a rust color. No, it was rusty, that was it.

She got some polish and a cloth and began to clean it, and she found that when the rust came off so did the black color. The key was really silver, and very beautiful. She wondered what it would unlock, and how she would find out. She decided to hang it on the chain with the stone, but as soon as she did so she had the feeling that the key was lighter than it had felt in her hand. Glancing at the nearby mirror she was shocked to find that neither key nor stone were there. In a panic she clutched the chain. Yes, they were there, she could feel them, but they had become invisible. How very strange! Why had they? What did it mean?

Still, she felt somehow comforted for no real reason, and when she went to bed she went straight to sleep. She dreamed that Rowan was in her woodland cottage, busily at work at a spinning wheel, singing as she spun. It was a good dream, and when it passed she slept on, smiling in her sleep.

Chapter Four
The Dwarf

Many months rolled by, but Rowan never returned to her cottage in the palace garden, or sent any message to Neva. If Neva had been able to slip away into the forest, as she used to do when she was younger, she would have gone in search of Rowan's home and maybe asked wayfarers for word of her. But now that she was twelve she was kept very busy with lessons and duties, and it was impossible to get away on her own. On her thirteenth birthday she was sent to stay with a famous voice teacher for ten months. Dame Alia was delighted with her and lamented the fact that she was a princess.

"Even if you were the child of the commonest charcoal burner, I could make you great and famous. But since you are a king's daughter I can only teach you to sing for your own pleasure and that of your friends."

Neva didn't mind. She had no desire to be famous, and singing for pleasure was all she cared about. She was glad to get back to Verlain and to her father. On the night of her return there was a great banquet, and she sang for him some of what she had learned. He was delighted.

"I have never heard anyone sing so beautifully except the Princess Melyni," he said. "I must persuade her to visit us, and the two of you will sing together like nightingales."

"I would like to hear her," Neva said, "and to see her. They say she is so beautiful."

"There is none fairer," said the king, his eyes kindling. "Her hair is like a flame and her eyes are like jewels and her cheek like the palest pink rose. When she smiles even the sunlight grows brighter. Yes, she must certainly come. You will love her."

Neva said nothing, but a little cold finger seemed to touch her heart. It had been over a year since her father had seen Princess Melyni. Yet he remembered her that vividly.

But that evening, as she was sipping her nighttime posset while her maid Silvi brushed her hair, she discovered that it had not been that long since the king had met the dark princess after all.

"How good it is to have you back, princess," said Silvi, "and how nice that your father is home, too. The court seemed so empty with both of you gone."

"Both of us? Was my father away?" she asked, surprised.

"Did you not know? He went to the Kingdom of Prayn to a great feast the Princess Melyni made in honor of something – no one is sure what. Some occasion in her kingdom. He was gone for nearly two months."

Two months? To attend a banquet at a castle less than three days' journey away?

Silvi said, "There was a storm after he got there, one that lasted days, and the roads were bad to travel on, so he was obliged to stay."

For two months? Neva set aside her posset, which suddenly tasted bitter. She said, "He thinks the princess is very fair."

"Yes," was all Silvi said.

Later, in her great carved bed with the pale green canopy above her, Neva lay awake, thinking. She wanted very much to have someone to talk to about the worry weighing on her heart. Not her maids: they loved her, but they would just try to soothe her with kind lies. And not Mother Desma or Master Piers. Someone like Prince Liam. But she did not feel that she could not write to the son of the High King and say, "I'm worried about my father and Princess Melyni." Although she had twice received letters from him in the year after her twelfth birthday, and had answered them, it had been a long time now since she had heard from him. Perhaps he had forgotten the friendship that had sprung up between them.

She wanted Rowan. She needed her. Why had Rowan gone away and deserted her? It was so strange. So frightening. It didn't make sense.

Fingering the stone and the invisible key, she suddenly made up her mind. Early in the morning she was going out into the woods in search of Rowan. She would leave a note for Linet and Silvi, so they would not worry. They would tell Master Piers, and he would be annoyed, but what could he do? Her father, having been away so long, would be busy with affairs of the kingdom, and Master Piers would not like to bother him unless it was necessary. And she would be back before dark, before anyone had real cause to worry.

35

With her mind made up she was able to sleep, and when she opened her eyes the silver of dawn was just creeping into the chamber. Getting into her plainest gown and most sensible shoes, she listened for sounds from her maids' room, but they slept soundly. At the last minute she took her little dwarf-made basket, attaching it to her belt. It might come in handy somehow.

She hadn't been out through the secret door since Rowan had gone away. She found the stairs very dusty. If the door was magic, the staircase didn't seem to be – at least not the kind of practical magic that would keep itself clean. Once outside in the dew-chilled garden she hurried, pausing at the cottage where Rowan used to stay. But it was empty, as always. Beyond it was a gate which opened directly into the woods. She stepped through and swung it shut behind her, and stood there a moment, her heart beating rather quickly.

She had often been out in these woods with Rowan, but never alone. There were no dangerous animals, not for miles around the castle. There were squirrels and rabbits and birds, and even a few deer, but the bears and wildcats had been cleared out in her grandfather's time. They lived now in the wild forests of the mountains, far away. But that was not to say the woods were perfectly safe. Rowan had said that, once, and when Neva had asked why, Rowan had replied, "No area that has ever been home to the Faerie is truly safe, not to the foolish or unwary. Even now, when few of us are left, things are sometimes not what they seem. People must walk carefully here."

"Well," said Neva aloud, as if answering that long ago warning, "I will walk carefully then. I have the stone and the key, and I want to find you, Rowan."

She set off up the twisting path that wound in among the thick trees with their low-hanging branches, glistening in the honey-pale sunlight which was replacing the coral of dawn. Birds were singing joyously and the early breeze was pleasant, and as she walked she sang softly, one of the songs from the book the prince had given her.

At first she hurried, in case Silvi or Linet, missing her, should send someone to fetch her back. Linet's husband Madoc knew these woods well, since he was a forester, and he and Linet would surely guess where she had gone. But as the morning slipped by and no one came after her, Neva walked more slowly. She passed the cottage where Madoc had once lived before he moved to court to wed with Linet, and where he had taught Neva to handle a bow. No one lived there now. Later still she passed the well where Rowan had once introduced her to a naiad. Perhaps the naiad was still there, but Neva did not stop. She felt that calling on one of the Old Spirits without invitation was rather impolite.

The sky was deep blue, now, but it was only visible in patches, so thickly did the trees grow. Sunlight lay in shivering droplets on the narrowing path as the leaves moved restlessly above it. The woods were wilder, but birds still sang, and once in awhile she would see a rabbit on the path, looking at her shyly but without fear. A squirrel called an impudent greeting from the branches of an oak tree, and Neva laughed back at him. But she was beginning to get tired, and she didn't know exactly where she was. Rowan had never brought her this far.

After awhile the path widened, and the trees opened up to make a small clearing beside a pool of crystal water. And sitting beside the pool, eating bread and cheese, was a man about three feet high. From his height and his muscular build and his rich brown beard she knew that he was a dwarf – the first she had ever met.

He stood up at once and bowed low. "Greetings, little lady," he said in a deep, pleasant voice.

Neva made her best curtsey and replied, "May the One smile upon this meeting," which was what a princess was taught to say to any member of another species on a first meeting.

"I am Thunel, son of Redstol, son of Braldor King of the Dwarves," said the dwarf.

Thunel! The craftsman, the one who had made her basket! Neva was delighted.

"I am Neva, daughter of King Verl of Verlain," said Neva, "and I am very pleased to meet you. My godmother spoke of you once, and I have something you made. But I never thought I would be lucky enough to meet you myself."

"You have one of my baskets," he said. "I only made two like that, one for the High Queen of the Southern Kingdoms, one for the Lady Rowan of the woods. So you are Lady Rowan's goddaughter."

Neva had never heard Rowan called Lady before, but it pleased her. Plainly, the dwarf saw beyond the peasant clothing to the true Rowan.

"Yes," she said. "Have you seen her lately?"

"Not for several years. Why do you ask?"

"Because she has disappeared. I am out looking for her now."

"Disappeared? The Lady Rowan? This is a hard surprise! Will you tell me more of this? Sit down and join me in my lunch, if plain food such as I have is not too harsh for you."

Neva promptly accepted the invitation. She was hungry, and the bread and cheese looked very good. As they shared Thunel's lunch she told him everything – about her father's wound, and the Princess Melyni, and how Rowan had gone but not returned. Then, because it was easy to talk to him, and he seemed interested, she went on to tell him the rest of her worries about Melyni and her father.

"So I have come to search for Rowan's cottage and see if I can find her," she finished. "I need her advice. It worries me that she has stayed away like this."

The dwarf shook his head and said nothing for a long while. At last, packing away what they had not eaten of the bread and cheese, he said, "I can direct you to her cottage. I know it well. But I have a heavy heart over this matter. The Lady Rowan has power, but there are others who have power, also, and some who have no love for her. The dark house of Prayn has reason to bear her a grudge. She brought about the downfall of the Witch Queen Kilse. I like it not that she went there, and was never seen again."

Neva drew in a deep breath. "You don't think they could have..." Her voice trailed off. She couldn't say the dreadful words.

"She is alive," said the dwarf quickly. "You can be sure of that. The death of one such as Rowan would have plunged all nature into mourning. The whole forest would know, up to the far end of the mountains. And I cannot believe any prison or dungeon could hold her. But there are spells – they say the queens of Prayn had great skill at entrapping even the Old Spirits of nature."

Neva thought of the magic mirror. She thought of Rowan being trapped in something like that, forced to come and go, and serve greed and vanity. She put her face in her hands.

"I can't bear to think of it! Oh, I won't believe it, not until I have to! Not Rowan!"

"Princess Neva," said Thunel after several moments, "you must be brave. I think you will need all your courage in the months to come, because I think hard times are approaching you. Word is out that Princess Melyni and your father are to be married. I tell you this because it is best to know the whole truth, however dark. It has not been formally announced, but my father heard it from one who is close to the dark princess. Melyni has always wanted the throne of Verlain. It may be that she incited the giants to attack the borders in the first place, in order to get your father into her power. Who knows?"

"Everyone says she has renounced witchcraft." Neva looked up, trying hard to be rational. "They say she swore fealty to the high king. I have tried to believe it."

"Many people have tried to believe it," said Thunel dryly, "but it is somewhat like trying to believe that the great dragons of the mountains will not breathe fire. Witchcraft is born into the daughters of the House of Prayn. They cannot renounce it. They can only refuse to use it, and Melyni, with her pride and vanity, is not likely to do that. Even if she has nothing to do with Lady Rowan's disappearance, she is not to be trusted."

"But what can I do? If my father loves her I cannot hurt him by letting him know I don't trust her."

"Your father is enthralled by her. As for love, that is something else. How enthralled no one knows, but it would be well for you to pretend friendship to her, anyway. I will give you one piece of advice, because I think you need guidance, young as you are, and with the Lady Rowan gone. If this thing truly comes to pass, and he brings Melyni to Verlain as queen, try not to look your best in front of her. Or to sing, either. I have heard that your voice is as lovely as your face, and she will not like that, not at all."

Neva was sure she wouldn't feel like singing much, if her father married Princess Melyni. As for not looking her best, she didn't think she would feel like wearing festive garments or weaving gold into her hair, or anything else of the kind.

"It is kind of you to give me advice," she told the dwarf. "I will try to follow it. And perhaps Rowan will come back, perhaps she is just away, busy with something. I want to visit her cottage today, anyway, in case she left some kind of message for me. Is it far?"

"Only a mile or so now. Follow the creek and you cannot miss it. As for me, I must travel on. I have things to sell in Roldene, and then I must head homeward, to attend the wedding of my cousin Kelvis in the mountains. But I am glad we met, and I will keep you in my mind and speak of you to the One."

Neva thanked him. He told her how to find Rowan's cottage, said goodbye and went on his way. He was lost from view among the trees almost at once. Moving slowly in the direction he had pointed out, Neva felt a sense of comfort in his promise of prayer. She would need all the prayers of friends in the days to come.

Chapter Five
The Wedding

She found the cottage without difficulty. She knocked on the door, though she did not expect an answer. Then she tried the latch. It lifted easily and she entered a small, sunlit room, with a neatly made bed in one corner, copper pans hanging above the fireplace, and a table with a bright cloth in the center. It was orderly and cozy, but everything was thick with dust. Rowan had not been there for a long time.

Neva walked all around the room. She did not feel as if she were trespassing, as she normally would have felt in someone's home during their absence. She felt as if she belonged. She opened cupboards as naturally as if they were her own. They held plain dishes and neatly labeled stone crocks of preserves and drawers containing herbs. The last cupboard, however, was locked. She passed it by, then stopped and went back. Taking the key from around her neck she tried it in the lock, and it went in easily and turned.

It will open doors for you if ever you need them opened. That was what Rowan had said so long ago. Therefore there was something in this cupboard that she needed. So it was a disappointment to find only a small brown box, half the size of her basket, and inside the box only a scrap of parchment. But when Neva took it out she saw musical notes written on it. It was two bars only, a very simple tune. She hummed it softly, half expecting something to happen, but nothing did. But it was a lovely haunting tune, and after a moment she put the parchment and the box into her basket. She couldn't have said why, but she somehow felt that the music had been left for her. Then she locked the cupboard door, and turned away. She was no nearer to knowing where Rowan was than before, but somehow, as she shut the cottage door behind her, she felt better.

It was almost sunset when she got back home and she found, as she had expected, everyone in a fluster of panic about where she had gone. Her father had half the guard out searching for her. He was very angry when she said she had gone for a walk in the woods and forgotten the time, but she said she was sorry so many times and promised so earnestly not to do it again that he at last forgave her.

"You are a princess," he reminded her. "You cannot go off on adventures like any country maiden. I know you are lonely, sometimes, and you miss Rowan. But I hope that very soon you will be lonely no more."

She looked up at him anxiously. She had been kneeling on the bottom step of his throne; now he reached down and drew her up to sit in her own small chair beside his.

"I have something to tell you, Neva," he said. "Something that I hope will make you as happy as it has made me. The Princess Melyni has done me the honor of promising to become my wife."

Neva silently thanked the One that this news did not come as a complete shock to her. She was able to take it without showing the sick feeling that curled in her stomach. But she could not speak.

"I know it is a surprise to you," her father said after a moment. "I would have prepared you if I could, but until I visited her at the Shadow Feast I had not made up my mind. I have thought much of her, and I have felt that you need a mother, especially as you grow into womanhood. But marriage is not a thing to enter into lightly. I loved your mother very much, Neva. I wed her for love alone and never regretted it. Yet there is something to be said for an alliance with a strong kingdom such as Prayn."

Neva took a deep breath and found that she could speak without her voice trembling.

"Do you mean you are going to marry her to strengthen your kingdom?"

"Not that alone. I could not marry someone for whom I had no regard. She is lovely and warm of heart, and we are both very lonely people. I do not love her as I loved your mother – I could never love that way again. But I love her in a different way. You are too young to understand as yet, but someday you will learn that there are many kinds and degrees of affection."

"I think I understand now," said Neva carefully. "Father, I will get used to this. I want you to be happy, truly I do. But I – I do not know her and it is – well, it is a surprise."

He patted her hand. "I know. But believe me, you and she will be dear friends. You will sing together, and you will have someone to talk to about things women do talk about. Before long

45

you will have suitors coming to court you, and what a help it will be to have a mother to advise and protect you!"

Neva had never thought much about being courted. It seemed worlds away. And from all she had heard about Melyni, it seemed unlikely that she would be someone to confide in.

But she murmured, "Yes, I suppose so," and tried to smile.

"A formal announcement of the wedding will be made tomorrow," said the king. "Until then, say nothing to anyone, not even your maids."

She promised, and managed soon to escape to her room. She was very quiet as her maids prepared her for bed, so quiet that they thought she had received a scolding from her father for her prank of the day, and even Mother Desma did not scold her any further. She was glad when she was alone, staring up at the canopy over her bed. It was a very long time before she was able to sleep.

The King's Council was the first to hear the king's announcement of betrothal the next morning. Later Neva heard the result of that. King Verl's mildness was such that none of his councilors had ever feared to speak their minds, and on this occasion they all spoke them, and at great length. No one was pleased. They reminded the king of the reputation of Prayn, of all the dark things attributed to the Witch-Queen Kilse, of her oath of vengeance when the king had passed over Melyni to marry Varena years ago. They agreed that the king needed a wife, and brought up names of all the eligible, respectable princesses, queens, and duchesses in the Southern Kingdoms. They complained that such a weighty decision should have been debated in council before it was made. But in the end nothing they could say moved the king from his decision. That afternoon the royal heralds went out to announce to the kingdom that King Verl and Princess Melyni would be wed in six month's time.

"So soon!" said Linet dazedly. "Why so soon?"

It was, in those kingdoms, customary for a royal betrothal to last a year, sometimes two. But, as Silvi pointed out, King Verl and Princess Melyni were not children or unknown to each other (as the case often was) and had no real reason to wait. All the same...

Neva's maidens had heard the decree almost before the council had finished debating it, and none of them could even pretend to be glad. Mother Desma, shaken from her usual complacency, could do nothing but weep. Most of the others seemed too stunned to even talk, which showed, Neva thought miserably, the degree of the impact the news had on them. They looked at her in a frightened kind of way; but Linet said to her fiercely, "I will look after you. No matter what happens. No one will have a chance to hurt you!"

This was even less comforting than the silence and tears. But Neva felt driven to put on a strong front and show loyalty to her father.

"Princess Melyni has sworn allegiance to the High King, and she and my father love each other," she said. "I will welcome her. She may not be as bad as people think."

But Mother Desma, the only one of them who had ever seen the dark princess, only shook her head and went on weeping.

Almost at once changes began to take place in the palace. Queen Varena's rooms were being redecorated for the new queen, and some of her own people came to oversee the task. They were arrogant and overbearing, and the master builder was very secretive about a certain chamber they were creating at the top of the tower. When Neva asked her father about it he could only say that Princess Melyni valued her privacy and had asked for this one room where no one would be allowed to go but herself. He did not seem concerned about it, but Neva wondered if the room would contain instruments of magic.

A couple of weeks later the new queen's personal effects began to arrive. Neva saw a lovely harp made out of some white substance like ivory, with strings of pure gold. It was placed in the secret chamber, which seemed a strange place for a harp. There were other musical instruments, however, made of the usual woods and metals, which were placed in the great room which joined Neva's chambers with the queen's. It was a large room, used by all the ladies of the court for music, needlework, and other daily activities, and there seemed to be no ban on anyone touching these instruments. Neva tried them all out. They had a richer, more lovely sound than any she had used before.

One day a letter came for Neva herself from the Princess Melyni. It was embroidered, not written, in red silks on fine fabric, and the scroll was tied with satin. The kingdom of Prayn, she thought, must be wealthier than Verlain.

"Dear child," said the letter; "your father has told me much about you and I am so anticipating meeting you at last. I have never had the opportunity to see very much of children, but I know we will be friends. I have things I can teach you, which you cannot learn from servants and maids of honor, however dear to you they may be. I hope you will love me as I know I will love you. I am sending you a ring which was mine when I was a child, and which every princess of Prayn has worn in turn. Since I have no daughter of my own, I pass it on to you."

It was signed with affection.

"She writes as if I am a child," said Neva to Linet. "Do you suppose my father forgot to tell her my age? But it is a good letter. It is kind of her to send the ring."

It was a gold ring, set with a dark ruby. It was very small, but Neva was able to wear it on her little finger.

That same day a second messenger arrived with a letter for Neva. This time it was from Prince Liam. There was a good deal of excitement over it, for he had not written for a long time, and Neva herself was curious. He wrote as if it had been but yesterday when they had last seen each other.

" I have been on a quest to free the people of the Northern Kingdoms from a gryphon that was terrorizing the Zeloyn Dukedom, and so I did not hear of your father's approaching marriage until I returned yesterday. I know you will not have forgotten the conversation we had about Princess Melyni. Neva, if you find things changed in any way after your father's marriage, come to us here. My mother will welcome you, and so will my sister Lannia. Only send us word and I will come myself to escort you."

Then he wrote of other things, of the gryphon he had subdued and bound with spells that would keep it from ever returning to terrorize the people again – Neva was glad he hadn't killed it, though her maids of honor assured her that most gryphons deserved to be slain – of the victory ball the Duke had given him, of the betrothal ball for his sister which was planned for Midsummer, of the small musical instrument called a klionna which the Zeloynians had invented and played on beautifully. He reminded her that he was ever her friend, and signed it informally with only his use name Liam.

Neva could not keep the letter from her father – she could think of no excuse for doing so. But fortunately he took the obscurely worded warning well.

"It is kind of His Highness to recall that daughters are sometimes not so comfortable with a father's second marriage," he said. "But of course it will not be like that with you, as you do not remember your own mother. I did not realize that you and he were such friends, my dear," he added.

"We became friends when he was here for my birthday," she said. "I had not heard from him for a long time. But they say his father never forgets a friend, and it seems the prince is the same."

She placed the letter in her special treasure box, but Princess Melyni's she had framed and hung up. It was so beautiful, and besides, she wanted to do everything she could to please her new stepmother.

And then the day came that the Princess was to arrive. Neva, standing on the battlements, watching the highway that wound through the hills and passed by the village before climbing to the royal palace of Verlain, was the first to see the great cloud of dust approaching. It was larger than she had expected; it looked more like the approach of an army than of the usual dozen or so guards who would escort a visitor. But before long she saw the black banner, embroidered in silver with the leopard couchant that was the emblem of the House of Prayn. She hurried down to join her father in the throne room.

It was still almost an hour before the captain of the guard came to the throne room, threw open the bronze doors, and announced, "Her Most Glorious Highness, Princess Melyni of Prayn!"

She entered unescorted and swept across the room in a gown of the richest shade of green, glittering with diamonds that matched the diamond tiara in her flaming hair. Neva couldn't help gasping. She had been prepared for a beautiful woman, but not as beautiful as this. Her hair was like beaten copper, her face like that of a goddess in a marble statue, save that instead of marble whiteness it was peaches and cream. Her eyes were as green as emeralds under delicately arched brows, and her lips were soft and more crimson than Neva's own. Surely she must be the most beautiful woman in the world!

The king went to meet her, moving like one in a dream, and Neva did not blame him.

"My lady," he said, kissing her hand. "Welcome! It has been so long!"

"Every day was like a year to me, also," she murmured in a low, rich voice. "But our period of waiting is almost at an end."

Then they seemed to remember that they were not alone. King Verl led his bride-to-be to the foot of the throne where Neva stood, entranced.

"My daughter Varena Alysha Anet Lilias, called Neva," he said formally.

Shock brought Neva abruptly out of the spell. Except at christenings and funerals the full names of royal persons were never spoken. It was considered bad luck and possibly dangerous for any but the parents and the bishop who had christened them to even know what the names were. It wasn't, of course, impossible for anyone to learn them, for they were recorded in the Royal Book, which was kept in the Cathedral of Verlain. But anyone seeking to do so would have been regarded with suspicion. It was unheard of for a princess to be presented by her full name.

Princess Melyni seemed startled, too, as she and Neva regarded each other; startled and somehow displeased. Then she smiled, but it was a rather hard smile.

"You are much older than I realized, Princess," she said, a slight bite to her words. "And beautiful," she added in almost a whisper.

"Oh, no!" Neva exclaimed. "It is you who are beautiful!"

There was such sincerity in her voice that Melyni smiled. "Well, I thank you," she said in a normal pitch of voice. Then she turned to smile at the king. "Verl, you led me to believe your daughter was a child!" she said playfully. "Why, she is almost a woman! It is indeed time she had a mother!"

"The years go so quickly," he said. "But she is child enough still. She likes to play in the woods. I have had to tell her she must not do that anymore. But now that she has you, she will have other things to occupy her mind."

"Yes," said Melyni. "She will."

And again there was a slight bite to what she said.

Princess Melyni had brought, as Neva had seen from the battlements, a large company with her; not only men-at-arms, but also an entire household of ladies and servants, with all their possessions. Neva, who had at first thought that the household of Prayn had only come for the wedding, soon discovered that they had come to stay. The princess explained to King Verl that they had all been with her for many years, and she could not bear to part with them. He at once agreed that places would be found for them all.

"And how that is to happen, the One above only knows!" grumbled Mother Desma that evening as she prepared Neva's bath. "Some of us will be sent away to make room for them, you mark my words!"

She grumbled under her breath, however, for six of the newcomers were in the room. They were to attend Neva.

"Father will not send any of you away!" Neva protested. "Why, you have been with me for many years, too."

But she was worried. It was easy to see that the king was so besotted with the red-haired princess that he hardly knew his own mind.

The next day was the wedding.

King Verl had wanted to have a grand affair, with all the rulers of the Kingdoms present. But Melyni had pleaded for a small, quiet wedding, which seemed so unlike her that it made Neva uneasy. Even the ladies from Prayn were disappointed and surprised. They at first blamed Verl, but at last were convinced that it was their own ruler's wish, after which they became silent on the subject. It was clear that they were devoted to her.

"Or frightened of her," Linet muttered, but only Neva heard.

So there were only ten in the wedding procession, which walked from the main palace to the great cathedral near the castle gates along a way lined with cheering crowds. Small children went first, scattering flowers along the great crimson carpet that had been laid along the road. Next came Neva, wearing a magnificent dress of satin and velvet, on which the dressmakers had worked day and night to get ready for her. Her father had chosen the pattern and color. Neva would have preferred a simpler gown of pure white instead of this elaborate one the color of old gold, and set with precious stones. As Neva walked before the bride and groom she had no idea what, if any, impression her gown had made on her stepmother, but she did know that it had drawn gasps of admiration from all the ladies this morning, and that some of them had looked troubled.

Around her neck was a heavy pendant set with pearls, but also around her neck she wore the invisible key and stone, and they felt reassuring to her.

The highest nobles of both courts followed Neva, and then came the royal couple, followed by other attendants. The shouting of the people and the weight of her dress and jewelry made Neva's head ache, even before they reached the cathedral. Then there was the three-hour ceremony and the procession back afterwards. By the time the wedding feast was drawing to a close, Neva was exhausted. And there was still dancing and entertainment to follow.

She had a brief rest and was able to change into a more comfortable dress after the feast, however. Linet bathed her head with cool, perfumed water, took the pins out of her hair and combed it out loose, held only with a light silver circlet.

"Perhaps I shall not have to stay long," Neva thought as she re-entered the Great Hall, cleared now of all tables save the high table on the end dais, where the newly wedded couple sat. There was an empty chair for her beside the bride. Melyni, too, had changed from her bridal garments, and now wore green velvet, which set off her flaming hair to perfection.

Up in the musician's gallery the music was beginning, and around the edges of the room the courtiers waited for the king's signal that the dance might begin. At last he rose and spoke to Lord Aimson, the herald, who was master of ceremonies. Lord Aimson moved to the center of the room and his great voice rolled out.

"Lords and ladies, before the dancing begins we will be favored by a song from our new queen."

There was loud applause. Nearly everyone had heard of Melyni's beautiful voice. Neva clapped louder than anyone, and her stepmother smiled at her before stepping down from the dais to sit at the harp which some of her people had brought out. It was not the ivory and gold one, but a smaller instrument, its graceful shape decorated with silver flowers. As she ran her fingers across the strings the hall grew very still.

The song she sang was in a language Neva did not know. But that didn't matter. The beauty of the deep, rich voice, weaving and intertwining with the notes of the harp, held her spellbound. It did not matter what she was singing. All that mattered was that she should go on and on, and never stop. And yet – and yet –

Neva's hand brushed the stone at her throat and her head seemed to clear, and she was able to listen in a more detached fashion. Beautiful though it was, there was something not quite – not quite nice about it. Neva felt somehow uncomfortable, as if she had eaten too many sweetmeats, or breathed in too much heavy perfume. She wondered now what the words were, and if they were in the witch-language of Prayn. She wondered if they were a spell. Glancing at her father she saw that his eyes were fixed upon his bride as if no one else existed.

When the song ended there were cries of protest and pleas for more. But Melyni shook her lovely head, smiling, and called out, "I thank you. But let us hear from someone else now. I understand my new daughter is something of a singer. Come, Neva, give us a song!"

Neva shrank back. She usually loved to sing. But she couldn't sing like that. Her songs were usually springtime ballads of love, and woodlands, and the faerie. Even the songs of the sea folk which she had learned from the music Prince Liam had given her were not the songs of allure that some said the merfolk sang, but clean, fresh, outdoor ballads of the sea and the stars. Besides, she remembered too well the warning of the dwarf Thunel. Do not sing in front of her, he had said.

"I cannot sing," she stammered. "My – my throat hurts."

But they would not accept excuses. Her own people, pleased to show the Prayn courtiers that their own little princess was talented, too, were calling for her, and her father, smiling, was saying, "Go, Neva. I have bragged so much of your voice that they all want to hear it."

Reluctantly she went down and sat at Melyni's harp. The queen, smiling, said, "You can play it, I am sure. Or would you prefer to be accompanied by another musician?"

"I can play it," said Neva, avoiding her eyes. Did Melyni want her to fail? Or did she truly want to hear her, with no dark intent?

Neva drew a breath, swept her fingers across the strings, and began to sing the first thing that came into her mind. It was a simple song, one she had learned as a child from Rowan.

Dancing stars in vaulted sky; praise the One.

Daisy stars with golden eye; praise the One.

Bird and beast and wind and sun praise the Name.

All nature until time is done praise the Name.

The words were repeated in different sequences, her voice changing to correspond with each singer named, the bright, happy tune and the pure sweetness of her young voice filling the room. As if she brought sunlight, starlight, wind, and birdsong into the hall people lifted their heads, breathing deeply, smiling from sheer pleasure. The intoxication of Melyni's song was swept away. Men and women remembered their childhood, and summer days outdoors. When the song ended there was even greater applause than for the queen, and cries for more.

"Sing the song of the Mermaid Zethira, daughter," called the king.

Neva would rather not have sung that one, which was the most difficult of the sea songs, and took all her breath and training. Any child might have sung the praise song, she thought; it could not possibly have offended Melyni. But this...

One cannot refuse a royal command, even from one's father, so she bent her head submissively, stood, lifted her face and began to sing. In the sea the merpeople played harps, or so she had heard, but no land instrument could reproduce the sounds to go with their music. It was for voice alone. As she sang she felt the wind and the salty waves, though she did not really know what the words meant, only the emotions they conveyed. She imagined herself, not the snow singer her people affectionately called her, but a mermaid floating on the green sea, waiting for the merlord she loved. The room around her faded as she sang, and she put her whole self into the images she visualized.

There was an awed silence when she finished. Some of the ladies were weeping, she saw. Not until she smiled and turned back to the high table did the shouting and applause break out, wilder and more enthusiastic than it had been for the queen. And Neva, looking at her stepmother, knew that she had made a great mistake. Royal command or no, she should not have sung that song. She should have pretended that she had forgotten it, or pleaded a headache, or anything at all. The new queen's eyes were no longer green but dark as coals and her face was sheet white.

She looked evil and dangerous, all the more so because she smiled. Neva sat down, trembling, and did not look at her again.

The dancing began after that. Neva danced with the lords she was obliged to dance with, glad not to have to sit beside her stepmother and make conversation. She danced all evening, until the royal couple bade their subjects good night and went to their bridal chamber. Then Neva also left the hall, feeling more exhausted than she had ever felt in her life. As Linet and Silvi prepared her for bed they chattered about her songs and how lovely she had looked.

"Even the queen was impressed!" said Silvi.

Impressed? Neva wondered sleepily if she had only imagined that evil look in her stepmother's eyes. Perhaps she was being unnecessarily sensitive. But she was too tired to really think it over, even when she lay at last in her bed.

CHAPTER SIX

Although the wedding itself had been small, there were weeks of celebration afterwards. Guests came from all over the kingdoms and there were balls and masques and hunts and tourneys, but Neva had little to do with most of these. Except for an occasional appearance for the first hour of a ball, or at a tourney, she was occupied with celebrations especially arranged for the young people. There were several of them, Neva's age and younger who had come with their parents, and most of them, like Neva herself, were more interested in picnics, plays, and entertainments than tourneys and balls.

Melyni had put the choice to Neva the morning after the wedding, coming to Neva's own apartments to breakfast with her and discuss the coming weeks. Dressed in a plain blue morning gown, with her flaming hair braided down her back, she looked lovely but not at all alarming, and her manner was so pleasant that Neva was ashamed of her own fears.

"You see, my dear," she said, "many of the young people are still but children, and the others, like you, have not yet had much experience of balls and such. They would be bored, and besides, it is not good for children to mingle with adults at entertainments where there is rich food and wine. Some of the guests may drink overmuch, and the conversation may be ill for you and your guests to hear. So I think (and your father thinks also) that separate jollifications would be more appropriate. But the choice is yours.

You are on the verge of womanhood. If you would rather come to our celebrations, of course you may."

Neva quickly agreed that she felt more a child than a woman, and would undoubtedly have more pleasure in celebrations arranged for the youth. Melyni's manner became even warmer after that, and Neva knew she had made the wisest choice.

So there were plays and pageants and games, and Neva was agreeably surprised at how thoughtful and inventive her stepmother was in planning these. And every morning they breakfasted together, and often Melyni sent little gifts to her throughout the day.

"Can it be that she truly wants to be my friend?" Neva asked Linet. "I believe she truly loves my father, and perhaps she wants to love me for his sake."

"It may be so," Linet agreed but doubtfully.

By the time the first month, the honey-moon of the wedding, was over, Linet was the only one of Neva's usual attendants left, but the change had taken place so gradually and naturally that no one thought it strange. Mother Desma was of an age that it was not strange for her to be sent to live with her daughter and son-in-law with a pension. Silvi had been given an appointment at the Court of Prayn, which, though their princess now lived in Verlain with her new husband, was still that country's royal palace, and so needed a full staff. It was a far more important situation, and Silvi was flattered. The other maids of honor were moved or sent away in a like manner, one at a time, and their places were taken by ladies of good families, some from other kingdoms, most from Prayn. The woman who took Mother Desma's place was the Lady Gladulla, who was as capable but less fussy than Desma had been.

Even Master Piers, Neva's tutor, was sent away; Melyni said that Neva had more need to learn dance and diplomacy and court etiquette than languages and history.

like manner, one at a time, and their places were taken by ladies of good families, some from other kingdoms, most from Prayn. The woman who took Mother Desma's place was the Lady Gladulla, who was as capable but less fussy than Desma had been.

Even Master Piers, Neva's tutor, was sent away; Melyni said that Neva had more need to learn dance and diplomacy and court etiquette than languages and history.

"You are a princess, and will most likely be a queen one day," she said. "What need have you of book learning? That is for boys and men, particularly scholars or merchants or ambassadors. What a woman needs to know is how to use her beauty and charm to keep her household running smoothly."

Neva had never agreed with this. She felt that all knowledge was of value, even for a princess. But when she was with Melyni, everything her stepmother said sounded reasonable and the thought of arguing it never entered her head. It was very strange.

Another thing that was very strange was how seldom she saw her father. Unless she was bidden to sit with them at a joust or to open a feast, she never set eyes on him. When she did he seemed very taken up with his bride, though he always had a smile and a few words for Neva.

"It is always so during the first months after a wedding," said Lady Gladulla. "Never fear, your father loves you as always, but right now he is enchanted with his bride and wrapped up in her."

The honey-moon began to draw at last to a close. Some of the guests had departed. A good many of the children had gone, but Neva never seemed to have time to herself. She was never alone. Some of her maids were always with her, and Lady Gladulla saw to it that everyone was busy. She was teaching Neva how to embroider with a new and difficult stitch, which was fascinating. Still, Neva began to feel a vague restlessness. Mother Desma had been a fussbudget, but the rest of her maids had always let her alone when she wanted solitude. They had known her all her life, and understood her ways. Lady Gladulla seemed to think there was something wrong with anyone who wanted to be alone for any reason, and Neva was too gentle to assert her royal authority to get her own way.

The wedding had taken place in late February and the honey-moon should have ended in March. But there was, it seemed, a special holiday of Prayn which took place the first day of April, so the festivities were prolonged to include a celebration of that day. There was to be a great daylong excursion to the king's river palace, which was on an island, several hours away. The entire court was to go.

Neva awakened with a severe headache that morning. She was not accustomed to being ill and on this day of all days she wished to be up and about. She hoped it would go away if she lay abed a short while longer, but when Melyni came to have breakfast with her, it had not eased.

"My dear child!" Melyni exclaimed. "You should have sent someone to fetch me as soon as you felt ill. I have a potion that will ease your pain, but it might be well also if you kept to your bed today. I hope you are not very disappointed."

Neva *was* disappointed. She had hoped to have some time to talk to her father today, and besides she loved the river palace, especially in the spring. It was surrounded by woods, and the gardens were full of birds and butterflies and even rabbits sometimes. But she felt so ill that she knew she wouldn't really enjoy it.

The queen's maid Agathe brought the potion in a cup the color of a ruby, with some kind of embossed design on it. She had her cloak over her shoulders and was in hurry.

"You are to drink a third of it now, a third at midday, and the rest just before sunset," she said. "I have told your girl Linet but no doubt she will forget, flighty wench. You must remember. This is precious stuff."

"What is it?" Neva asked. "I know something of healing herbs myself."

"I do not know what is in it, it is a great family secret of the House of Prayn," said Agathe coldly, and swept out of the room.

Neva sat up. Through the window she could see the horses and carriages winding their way in procession out of the courtyard. A small body of guards would be left behind, and probably some kitchen and chamber maids; otherwise no one was left in the palace except Linet and Neva. She had told the rest of her maids to go. Why disappoint them? She would perhaps sleep all day.

She took the goblet from the table. The potion was dark in color and had no odor of any kind. She lifted it to her lips. As she did so, the bottom of the cup brushed the stone that hung invisible on its chain. All at once the cup began to vibrate in her hand, and the stuff inside began to give off an odor like old mushrooms, and to steam.

Startled, she held it away from her. The goblet had changed color, and instead of gleaming ruby red it was black as coal. The only red was in the embossed design which she saw now was a serpent. It seemed to writhe as if alive.

Neva put the cup from her, spilling some of it on to the carpet on the floor. Where the drops landed holes appeared, as if eaten by acid.

She sat very still, staring down. All at once her headache was gone, and her mind was perfectly clear, clearer than it had been for weeks. Poison. It was poison. Had it not been for her magic stone she would be dying at this moment. How could she have so forgotten herself as to trust the queen? It was as if she had been under a spell and was now free of it.

She got out of bed, carried the goblet carefully to the casement, and poured the contents out on to the cobbled courtyard below. She saw steam rising where it fell. Then it faded away and was gone.

Neva went out into the outer chamber, where Linet should have been sitting, but no one was there. She called, but there was no answer. She went into the dressing room, and took clothing and dressed herself in a plain grey gown and soft leather shoes, and then she started through the castle, looking for Linet. It felt strange

65

to be all alone. Had the queen planned this, too? Had she found some way of removing Linet, so that no one would come near Neva's bed until it was too late? Her heart was pounding hard. She thought of summoning the guards. But she knew that they were all Melyni's people. Nearly everyone in the castle had come from Prayn, now. How was it that she had not taken note before of the way the good old servants and courtiers of Verlain had been weeded out?

Footsteps sounded on the stairs coming from the queen's chambers. Before Neva could decide whether or not to hide, Linet came flying down the steps, white-faced and wild-eyed.

"Linet!"

"Your Highness! Oh, my lady!" The maid's breath was coming in gasps. "Come with me! Come and see what I have seen!"

"But what is it? Calm down, Linet! What has frightened you?"

After a few moments the maid's breathing became easier and she was able to make sense.

"Before she left Agathe asked me to get a certain gown from the Queen's bedchamber and mend it while they were gone. So I went up and – oh, my lady, come and see!"

Neva followed her up the short flight of stairs and into the queen's outer room, where there were elegantly carved and richly cushioned chairs. Neva had seen the room before, and also the boudoir where Linet led her. Beyond the bed, in the panelled wall, was the door opening on the tower steps, at the top of which was the private room. And it was open, open wide, the door flat against the wall, with light coming down from the chamber above.

"I should not have gone up," Linet gulped, "but it has never been open before, and there has been so much mystery about that chamber..."

"I do not blame you," said Neva.

Linet led the way up the steps, and Neva followed her up and into the secret room. It was large, much larger than she had realized, and richly carpeted and curtained in scarlet. Hanging on the wall was a mirror framed in gold, crystal clear and very beautiful. There were other things – the great white and gold harp, urns of marble and gold, cupboards and shelves – but the mirror drew them like a magnet. It hung against the farthest wall, and below it were carved words.

"Speak to me in rhyme or verse

"And what does that mean?" asked Neva uneasily.

"I do not know but I have heard of this mirror. Liva, who served as the queen's maid of honor before she became yours, says that it will answer any question, but that the queen asked it but one thing. Listen, Your Highness:

" Mirror spirit at my call

The mirror began to film over. Colors swirled in its depths, pink, yellow, green, until they came together to form a face, green-skinned with grave, purple eyes. A distant voice, like ice crystals striking glass, replied:

"Fairer than moon and brighter than sun

Then it faded away and the mirror was crystal clear again."That is what it said to me," said Linet, her voice trembling. "Oh, my lady, I am frightened! Liva told me the verse I said, the verse that Queen Melyni asks the mirror each morning. The spirit in the glass cannot lie, Liva says, and it has never told Queen Melyni anything but that she herself is the fairest of all. What will she do when she hears this answer? I have heard terrible stories of her temper, and of what she has done to any rival! They say she spent weeks casting evil spells on your mother when the king married her, but Rowan was here then, and was able to thwart them!"

Neva drew a deep breath. She thought of saying, as well she might, that the mirror, faced with Melyni's beauty, might have given her quite a different answer than it had given Linet, but she didn't believe it. She was sure that this explained the potion of this morning. Yet she felt surprisingly calm.

"She tried to poison me this morning," she said.

"Oh!" Linet's eyes were wide with horror.

"Luckily I spilled some of the potion, and saw that it ate holes in the carpet, and so I threw it away. Or I would be dead now. I don't know what she will do when she finds out she failed, but I also do not think I should wait to find out."

"But what can you do? Do you think – if we got a message to the High King..."

"I don't think I can wait even for that. And whom can we send? The castle is full of her people."

"Well... There is Madoc...."

There was a strange uncertainty in the maid's voice that made Neva look at her sharply. She was staring at the floor, chewing her lips.

" What is it, Linet? Madoc seems like a very good choice."

"Yes, only ... My lady, he trusts the queen. He thinks she is quite – quite wonderful." Linet's voice quivered slightly. "Only last evening we quarreled over it. He is – he is like one bewitched."

"And so he may be," said Neva, drawing a long breath. This was almost as hard for her to accept as it was for Linet. She had known Madoc all her life. He had been a friend of Rowan's, he had taught Neva how to shoot with a bow, and made toys for her, whittled out of wood.

"If he is, it is not his fault, Linet," she said, putting her arm around the maid's shoulders. "And I cannot believe that he would betray me to the queen, but we dare not take a chance. I must go to the High King myself. I must leave here today, while everyone is away."

"I will come with you."

Neva thought for a few moments. She felt that she would have a greater chance of escape on her own. She was young and agile; she could climb trees if there were need to hide, and she could travel on foot, at least as far as the Abbey of Evergrace at the foot of the mountains. The Father Abbot there would help her. But Linet was slow of foot and heavy, and would tire easily. On the other hand, leaving her to face the questioning of the queen was not to be thought of.

"Two are more easily tracked than one," she said, "but there is something you can do for me, Linet. Your mother lives near the Castle of Vonn, does she not?"

"Yes, at the very gate."

"There would be nothing odd, then, in my letting you go to visit her. I will write a note, saying that I gave you leave, just in case you are stopped and questioned. Do you remember the Countess Daril of Vonn? Her father died and she now rules the county there. Tell her what is happening here, and that I am trying to reach the High King. Ask her to send a message to Prince Liam, telling him about it. And ask for her protection; tell her that I said you were not to come back. Will you do that?"

"But, Your Highness, I cannot let you go off on your own!"

"I'll be all right," Neva said. "I will go through the woods as far as the Abbey, and the Father Abbot will surely be able to help me. I am safer in the woods than you know. Rowan is not forgotten there."

"In the nearer woods, yes, but you will have to go through the deep forest to reach the Abbey. And if you take the woods you must walk. How can you?"

"I have done more walking than you realize. Do not worry about me, Linet, just concentrate on not getting caught. Now go and put some things together for the journey. I will meet you in the sun room in a few moments."

Linet went, and Neva stood there for a few minutes, wondering if the mirror could give her advice on her journey. But the idea of compelling one of the Old Spirits to come at her call was so dreadful to her that she could not bring herself to try it. She looked around the room, feeling somehow unwilling to just go, as if there was something here that she needed, or that needed her. She thought of Rowan. Was Rowan here, trapped somehow, like the spirit of the mirror? The idea made her feel sick.

"Rowan?" she said shakily. "Are you here?"

There was no answer, but the room seemed to somehow grow more still, as if someone was listening.

"Rowan!" Neva called more strongly. "If you are here, show me how to set you free! Are you here?" Still nothing. Yet she felt as if she had not said quite the right words, or that she was forgetting something essential that would break through the silence.

She was almost out of the room when suddenly she thought of the tune she had taken from the cupboard in Rowan's closet. She stopped and turned back. It was silly, probably, and a waste of precious time but... She drew a breath and began to sing it. There were no words but she sang the notes, and as she sang something happened. Only she wasn't sure what. Either the room grew warmer or lighter, or some fragrance moved like a breeze around it. She sang it twice. Rowan did not appear. But somehow she felt more comforted than she had felt in a very long time. She had the feeling she used to have when she was very small, when Rowan used to come to kiss her goodnight with a murmured, "Sleep well, snow singer, and may the One keep you safe all the night." And Neva would drift off, secure in Rowan's blessing. She felt secure now. She must go. She must try to get to the High King and ask his help. But she wasn't frightened. Somehow it would be all right.

71

Chapter Seven
The Flight

Getting away was not so quick a process as Neva had hoped. First of all she wanted to make sure Linet got off safely, and that took awhile, mostly because Linet fluttered and dithered and kept bursting into tears as she packed. And then, once she was gone, Neva had to attend to her own packing.

Linet had found her a knapsack that had belonged to Madoc in his forester days, which was not too large for her, yet was surprisingly roomy. She packed food first. The kitchen was deserted, as she had expected. The servants were celebrating a day free of family and guests in their own hall. She found meat pies and cheese and bread and apples, and she added a flask of water.

She would have liked to take some money, too, in case she had to pay for assistance, but the treasury would be sure to be guarded. All she had in her own room, she found, was a small leather purse containing coins for tossing to the people as she rode out in procession. It was a gesture, only, because the people of Verlain were well taken care of, and there were no poor, so the coins were small ones. After a little thought she opened the top drawer of her bureau, where she kept her jewelry, and spent some time in desperate thought.

She did not want to take anything that had come from her stepmother. Jewels were too easily recognized, and Melyni certainly knew every piece she had given Neva. Even if they were not bewitched, they could be traced. And of her jewelry which had not come from Melyni, the only pieces of value had been her mother's. She had never worn them. Except for state occasions she had never had reason to deck herself out with expensive jewelry, and until Melyni came there had been few of these. But she often looked at them and thought about her mother.

Opening the sandalwood box where they lay, now, she gazed at them and remembered that morning, a week before her twelfth birthday, when her father had given them to her.

"You will soon be a young lady, no longer a child, my dearest," he had said. "I always meant to give you the things that were your mother's when you reached your twelfth year. You will not wear them yet, but soon you will be invited to balls and state events in other kingdoms, and you will find occasion to put them on."

He had ridden away that evening to fight the giants, and had fallen into Melyni's clutches. It had been their last intimate talk without her shadow to cloud it.

In the box was the ring set with rare pearls which had been Queen Varena's betrothal gift from her husband; earrings of beaten gold that the dwarves had made for her coronation, with a bracelet that matched; a silver pendant hung with a single diamond of rare value, which had been the gift of the High King and Queen; and several less valuable pieces, yet costly still. Many of them had been gifts from visiting royalty. They were of silver and gold, and could be exchanged and not traced as easily as the expensive pieces, so probably she should take only them. Yet it went against Neva's heart to leave any of her mother's jewelry behind, for her stepmother perhaps to find and wear. The sandalwood box was small.

In the end she decided to take everything. But before closing the box and slipping it into the pack, she took out the betrothal ring. She slipped Melyni's ring off her finger, tossed it among the tumbled pillows of her bed, and replaced it with her own mother's ring. She would wear it always.

She finished packing more quickly then, adding a change of clothing and a light cloak which could be rolled up and used as a pillow in need. She put a heavier cloak on over her gown, wishing she had access to boys' clothing. It would be easier to climb or run in. But she didn't, and what she had would have to do. At least both gown and cloak were old and shabby, country clothes which she had taken from Rowan's garden cottage. A casual by-passer would never guess that she was a princess – and nor would robbers, when she reached the deep forest.

In the end it was well past midday when she stole down the secret stair, crossed the garden, and passed out into the woods. She would have to walk quickly, and even so, she would never reach the abbey tonight. She would have to find shelter in the woods.

With a prayer to the One Who Hears, she set off at a good pace. She followed the path at first, since she would not be missed for awhile and it ran in the direction of the mountains. The sky had been blue and sunny this morning, but now it had begun to cloud over and the air was muggy. But the walking was still pleasant. Even if it rained later, her cloak had a hood, and the trees would help keep her dry. She found, to her own surprise, that she wasn't really frightened or unhappy. In her mind she knew that she was running for her life, and that she had probably left her home and her father forever. But her heart held only relief that she had escaped, and even a certain lightness. A sense of adventure, she thought, such as knights and princes must feel as they set off to battle dragons and giants. Dreadful things might lie ahead but her fate was in her own hands; she was no longer a helpless victim. She did wonder whether she should have brought a bow and arrows, but they would be bulky to carry, and anyway, she doubted if she could kill a living being, man or beast, even to save her own life. Shooting at a target was a very different thing.

After an hour or so she was no longer walking so quickly. The air was heavier, more oppressive, so that breathing was not easy, and she was growing tired. The woods were very quiet around her. No birds were singing, and there was no sign of rabbit or squirrel. Her sense of adventure was fading, and worries kept nibbling at her mind. She worried about Linet, about what her father would say when he found her gone, about what her stepmother would do. She worried about the unusual silence of the woods and the darkening clouds. They didn't feel natural. And she worried that she wouldn't get as far as she had hoped before nightfall.

At last she had to rest. She sank down into the grass by the side of a pool. She knew this spot. It was the naiad's pool, the one Rowan had introduced to her once when she was little. And there was the naiad itself, sitting on the surface of the water. It looked something like an old woman, but its hair was a waterfall and its face kept changing, like moving mist, so it was hard to look at. Neva jumped up and made her best curtsey.

"You have no time to rest, Princess," said the naiad. It had a warbly, splashy voice, like the voice of a brook. "You have been missed."

"Already?" Neva exclaimed in dismay.

"The moment you removed your stepmother's ring (a wise move) she knew that you had survived and were free of her spell. She told your father that some terrible thing had happened to you, and that they must return at once. They will be at the palace within the hour. She has already set her witchcraft in motion and a great storm is coming. You must find a hiding place soon."

"But where can I go?" Neva asked.

"That I cannot tell you. There are places of power in these woods, and even in the mountains, but you must find your own sanctuary. You have the blue stone that will defend you, but not against all things. You have the key that will unlock doors, but not all doors. You have your own courage and warm heart and sweet voice to win your friends. But still you are in great danger, for the Princess of Prayn has immense power. Put no trust in human beings. They can be manipulated."

"All human beings? But – but the High King – and Prince Liam..."

"The High King and his family have power of their own, and are beyond her reach. Your plan to seek their help is a wise one. But they are far away."

"Yes, I know," said Neva helplessly. She was becoming more frightened by the moment. The naiad's advice was not very helpful.

"Go forward, now, and seek shelter," the naiad said. "We who have some power will do what we can to confuse the searchers when they come, but in the end it will depend on you. Good fortune go with you, goddaughter of Rowan."

With a splash the naiad vanished, leaving Neva staring blankly at the pool.

Slowly she turned away and began to walk. She wished she had spent more time exploring these woods so she would at least have an idea where to go. Trust no humans, the naiad had said. Did that include the good monks at the abbey? Neva did not believe her stepmother could bewitch them, but they were, after all, subjects of her father's, and if he demanded that she be turned over to the Queen, could they refuse? He would never believe that his beloved wife meant to kill her, not even if the Father Abbot himself told him so. No, the naiad was right. She could not take the chance.

Anyway, she would never reach the abbey today, and her immediate concern was to find shelter now. The only safe place she knew of was Rowan's cottage. She was sure that no evil could touch her there. But could she reach even it before night, or before the storm broke? It was getting darker and darker. She willed herself to walk more quickly but it was as if some weight was slowing her down. Not far away she heard a low rumble. Thunder! Thunderstorms were as rare in the Southern Kingdoms as was snow in the winter. She could only remember two or three in her life, and she hadn't much liked them, even safe home with her maids around her. Out here in the woods she wasn't going to like it at all.

Then the wind came up, swaying the branches, and the thunder sounded again, closer. The rain began, cold and stinging, more like winter sleet than summer rain. She tried to run but she found herself only stumbling. There was thunder again, this time a loud crash right above her, and lightning split the sky. Neva came to a stop, so frightened she couldn't even move. She clutched the blue stone at her throat, whimpering softly without knowing that she was saying, "Rowan, Rowan, Rowan..."

There was another flash, a brighter one, but this time it sprang out of the bushes, not from the sky. A lovely, silvery form stood before her, pawing the ground, glistening mane shaking, and the light bounced off the long, fluted horn on its forehead. A unicorn! A real unicorn! And it spoke in a voice like light turned into sound.

"Follow!" it said. "Keep your eyes on me!"

It sprang forward, and Neva sprang after it, freed from that awful weight that had held her back. She could run now, keeping up with the glorious creature before her, and she was neither out of breath nor tired. Fixing her eyes on his silver tail she didn't see the lightning above her, and keeping her attention on his hoof beats she didn't hear the thunder. She followed him on and on, hardly aware of the wind and rain. Perhaps it was hours they ran, perhaps only minutes; she could not tell. But all at once he stopped, reared up, twirled once, and vanished. She gave a cry of distress, but it died almost immediately. She was standing in front of Rowan's cottage door.

Her fingers trembled as she unlocked the door. Inside she slammed it shut behind her and dropped the heavy crossbar into place. Then she stumbled over to the bed and sank down upon it.

Safe. She was safe. Here in the friendly darkness she felt as if Rowan's arms were wrapped protectingly around her. Nothing could harm her here. The storm could rage as it pleased, the darkness of her stepmother's arts could pound against the cottage walls, but nothing could get in. She was sure of it.

When her trembling had stopped she got up and looked for candles and lighted them. The shutters were closed, and she didn't think the candles gave off enough light to gleam through the cracks, even if there were searchers out in that storm. Anyway, she had to risk it. She needed enough light to get out of her wet clothing and find food in her pack. She hadn't eaten anything but a handful of grapes and a piece of cheese today, and that had been hours ago, this morning, as she helped Linet pack. She was very hungry.

As she ate a meat pie and sipped her water, she wondered if Linet had been far enough away to have missed the storm. If it was a magic storm, called up by Melyni, perhaps it had struck only the woods. In that case Linet must be almost to her mother's home by now. Perhaps she would see Countess Daril tonight. Tomorrow, anyway. And Daril would send a messenger to the High King. By the time Neva herself arrived there, the king would be expecting her. Perhaps Prince Liam would even set out to meet her. It was a cheering thought.

And it *was* a storm of black magic because even as she sat there the wind and rain stopped, not moving away, as normal weather might, but suddenly. The darkness became much less heavy, so much so that she blew out the candles, finding that more light came through the cracks than she had expected. It was evening light, a pale twilight. The clouds must have all passed away.

She was very tired. She put away what was left of the food, turned back the coverlet of the bed, and got under it. The sheets were warm, dry, and fragrant, despite the fact that they had not been used for over a year. Practical magic, she thought, smiling softly. She said a little prayer, closed her eyes, and was asleep.

Chapter Eight
The Forester

"Princess Neva! Princess Neva! Little snow singer, let me in."

The voice seemed to be right in her ear, whispering. She thought it had gone on for quite a long time before she began to wake up. It was a voice she knew, a friend's voice, but she was too befuddled with sleep to even be aware of where she was, never mind who it was. She lay blinking at the dark beamed ceiling. It was all she could make out in the dim light. Then, slowly, her mind began to clear and she remembered that she was in Rowan's cottage, hiding from her stepmother. And the dim light was moonlight, stealing through the cracks of the shutters.

"Let me in, little princess. Before they come. I will take you to safety."

And now she recognized the voice. Madoc! Madoc, who had been Rowan's friend, whom she had known all her life. Madoc, who used to tell her stories when she was little. Madoc, who had made her first harp. Madoc, who, unless his wife was wrong, now served the queen.

Could it be that Linet was wrong? Of course many people admired Melyni's beauty and charm and voice, but that did not mean that they were necessarily bound to do her will! Would Madoc really harm her? It was nearly impossible to believe, now that she actually heard his familiar voice nearby. Perhaps he had discovered the evil of the queen, and broken free of her spell. His companionship and assistance would make such a difference! He would escort her to the High King, protecting her against wild beasts and robbers along the way, helping her hide from the queen.

He had moved to the door. He was whispering through it now.

"Can you hear me, Princess Neva? Let me in!"

She sat up slowly. Purely from habit she cupped her hand around the blue stone. It became visible at her touch, glowing very faintly, as if lighted from within. It was icy cold in her hand. But what did that mean? Did its glow mean she could trust Madoc, or did the chill mean she could not? Who could tell?

Put your faith in no human beings. The words of the naiad sounded clearly in her head. No human beings. They could be manipulated. Yes, even old friends. Even humans who had known Rowan.

Slowly she lay back again. She could not take the chance. When all this was over, if it proved that Madoc had been faithful all along, he would forgive her, she was sure. But she dared not risk it.

He could not be sure she was here, though it was the logical place for her to have taken shelter. Even a magic storm would have wiped out her footprints – and at the speed with which she had followed the unicorn, she wasn't sure that she had even remained on the ground to leave footprints. She had been sleeping too soundly for him to have heard her move in the bed. No, he couldn't know, he could only guess. If she remained very still and did not answer, he would go away.

He moved around the cottage from window to door, calling her softly for a long time. But at last he left. She heard his footsteps moving off into the woods, and she let out a long breath. Would he go back to the queen and report that he had not found her at Rowan's cottage? Or would he join the other searchers? Or had he been on his own all along, trying to save her from the queen's wrath? There was no way of knowing, but Neva did know one thing. She must decide what to do now, and quickly.

By the amount of light stealing through the cracks there must be a full moon, and she felt rested, now, and refreshed. Should she go on, now, when no searchers were near? Her dark cloak would hide her if she kept to the shadows. No matter how bright the moon was, night was easier to hide in than day. No evil thing could touch her here, perhaps, but she could not stay here forever. Even if Madoc should report that she was not there, they would surely watch Rowan's cottage, expecting her to turn up, and would soon discover her. Then it would be simply a matter of waiting; her food would not last long, and she would have to come out.

But did she have the courage to go out into the night?

Well, she had to, that was all.

She sat up and slid to the floor, her feet tingling at the touch of the cold wood. Quietly she dressed in her spare clothes -- her others were still damp. She packed them so that they would not touch anything that the wetness would hurt. Then she stood, looking around the cottage in its dimness, hating to leave its safety and the subtle feeling of Rowan's protection. Her eyes rested on the sturdy door, with its crossbar firmly locking her in.

And then a cold rush of realization went through her. The crossbar! Of course Madoc must know she was here! He would have tried the door first thing and found it bolted from within! No wonder he had taken so long to give up! No wonder he had kept calling! And now he had gone – why? To tell his mistress that her stepdaughter was trapped in a cottage in the woods? It was even possible that they would not have to starve her out. Melyni might have ways, like setting the thatch on fire with lightning, for instance. Or, if she turned all her dark powers on the little house, could it withstand her, now that Rowan herself was not here? No, she had no choice. She must get away now.

When she stepped outside she blinked, startled. In spite of the light that had crept into the cottage, she had not expected this much brightness. The moon was full, resting in its star-studded velvet bed directly above the cottage, or so it seemed, sending floods of silver down into the woods. It would be easy to see her path. Of course it would be equally easy for her to be seen, but she would have to take that chance. She touched the blue stone for courage, and set off.

Although the leaves were so wet they glistened like diamonds, the path was muddy. Looking behind her she could see her own tracks, so she veered off the trail. The carpet of moss and old leaves and pine needles under her feet made only a gentle swooshing sound and left no mark. She was good at keeping a sense of direction, and she knew that she must go west. The High King's palace looked over the western sea.

But she soon found that keeping in one direction was difficult. Trees and bushes forced her to detour this way and that. Also, the patches of brilliant moonlight and sooty shadow were confusing, especially the shadows cast by the shifting branches in the soft breeze. She could only hope she was going in the right direction. She had the troublesome feeling that she was being followed, and kept looking back over her shoulder. Once she stopped to listen. The breeze had died down, and the wood was very quiet, as it had been before her stepmother's storm. She didn't like it. There should have been rabbits and other small night creatures rustling in the underbrush. She should hear an owl's hunting cry somewhere. Instead there was only the beating of her heart and the short panting of her breath.

And then suddenly there was a whizzing sound, and something went past her face, landing with a clunk. It happened so quickly that it was several heartbeats before she saw the arrow sticking out of the tree next to her and realized what had happened. She dropped flat, just as a second arrow struck the tree behind her, right where she had been a second ago. She wriggled frantically back into the bushes, taking cover among them, even knowing that they could not really save her. And indeed the marksman sprang out from his cover in the opposite bushes and took three long steps toward her. He had dropped his bow, and now held a long, glittering knife.

And it was Madoc. It really was. This awful thing was true.

She felt his big hand fasten around her arm, and as he dragged her out she screamed.

"Madoc! Madoc! No!"

She stared up at him and her heart stopped. It was the same rugged, handsome, familiar face that she had known since babyhood. Except for the eyes. Madoc's eyes were a warm blue, like a sky on a summer afternoon. These eyes were colder than the sapphires in her father's scepter, hard and glittering, with light bouncing off them. Eyes that were hardly human. Eyes that knew no mercy.

She closed her own, unable to bear it, so appalled at what Melyni had done to him that she almost forgot to be afraid for herself. She clasped the blue stone and waited for the blow but it did not come.

She opened her eyes again. He was staring at her as if bewildered, as if trying to remember something.

"Madoc!" she said on a gasp. "Don't kill me! Don't do that for *her*. Madoc, you are my friend. You are Rowan's friend. How can you do this?"

It was as if some mask suddenly shattered on his face. The hardness splintered and fell away, human light shone out of his eyes, light that turned into horror. He dropped his hands, the one holding the knife and the one gripping her arm.

"Princess Neva!" he exclaimed. "What am I doing? In the name of the One, what was I thinking?"

He flung the knife away. He reached down to lift her to her feet. She was trembling so much she could hardly stand, and tears were in her eyes.

"She bewitched you, Madoc," she said. "My stepmother. She sent you to kill me."

"Yes." He brushed sweat from his brow. "Now I remember. She said – it seemed so reasonable, so just and right – she said I must find and kill you – for her – because you wanted to kill her, and we must strike first — *You!* My princess, my little snow singer, as if

87

you would ever kill anyone! How could I..." Now there were tears in his eyes. "Then – I saw your ring – your mother's ring – It was as if I woke up from a dark dream..."

Neva let out a long, quivering breath, thanking the One that she had decided to wear the ring. She said, "I put on the ring before I left, and took all my mother's jewelry – I didn't want her to have it. She's evil. She's a witch."

Slowly he nodded. "Of course she is. Think who she is. I was afraid for you before she came. But when I met her, I..."

"Yes, I fell under her spell, too," said Neva. "I only snapped out of it this morning, when the drink she gave me turned out to be poison. I spilled some of it, and it ate holes in the carpet. So I ran away."

There was a fallen log nearby. Madoc stumbled to it and sat down. Neva sat beside him.

"Yes," he said finally, "she's evil, as was her mother, and her grandmother. But evil still follows some reasoning. Why does she hate you, little mistress? Why you?"

Neva felt extremely embarrassed saying, "Because her magic mirror says I'm more beautiful than she is." Instead she said, "She is a very jealous person. The night of the wedding feast when I sang, she was angry, and she has never forgiven me."

"She would have you murdered because you have a lovely voice?" Madoc sounded as if he couldn't believe it.

"Who understands a jealous heart? It sounds ridiculous to us, but everyone says she will stand no rivals in anything. But, Madoc, we must not sit here talking. I have to go on. I have to get to the High King; he'll protect me. How many people are out searching for me?"

"Right now, only I. She told your father that you had heard false things about her and fled, and that one person, such as I, who knows the woods and knows your ways, would have a better chance of finding and convincing you to go back, than a whole search party. But she told me that it was her life or yours, and that you must be destroyed. Little Princess, I do not know what to do next. I would escort you to the High King, but if I do not return, I fear that she will do something evil to Linet."

"Linet left this morning to visit her mother," said Neva. "I was worried about her, so I made her go."

He looked relieved. "Then we will travel together. But I must tell you that it will be a hard journey. When I do not go back to her, with proof of your death, she will turn all her dark magic against us. They say even the dragons of the mountains are under her sway."

"I don't believe that," said Neva, "but I do believe that she has great power. Now let me think a moment, Madoc, because we must make the right choice."

They sat in silence for a long while. It was a natural silence, though, Neva thought with part of her mind. The leaves were rustling, a deer bounded across the path, night creatures were stirring. Right now the evil was gone. But Madoc was right. If he did not go back, the queen would guess that her spell over him had been broken, and she would be furious. Who knew what she might do?

"We need time," she said finally. "And to buy it, you must leave me, Madoc. You must take to the queen some kind of proof that I am dead. And then you must get away – at once, before she can use her mirror or some of her other implements of magic. You must join Linet as quickly as you can. The Countess Daril will give you sanctuary. If Melyni is truly satisfied that I am dead she will be at her ease for a time, enough to give me a good start, even if it's only a day or two. But what can you take her?"

"I do not like to let you go alone, little snow singer. When you get into the deep forest there are wild animals. You will be torn to pieces!"

"I must risk it. Better to be killed by wild animals than killed by Melyni. Anyway, I am not really worried about wild beasts. I have a protection that you cannot see, given me by Rowan before she went away, and it still works. I was delivered from the storm yesterday. I don't think bears and wolves will hurt me."

This seemed to reassure him greatly.

"What proof of my death did she ask you to bring back to her?" Neva asked him.

He hesitated. Then he told her. "Your hair. She said I must cut off your hair and bring it to her as proof. Forgive me, Princess. It is a vile and humiliating thing, I know."

"It would be to her," said Neva and laughed aloud. "Don't look so unhappy, Madoc! She could have demanded my entire head, and then what would we have done? Can you cut my hair with your dagger?"

"I am certain I can, but Princess..."

"No, really, I don't mind! If it is short it will be out of my way. I may even be able to disguise myself as a boy if I can get some boys' clothing somewhere along the road. I know there is a village in the foothills where I might be safer as a boy. Now you look shocked. When one is adventuring, one must do what comes to hand, isn't that so? Let us not worry about a little hair! It will grow back."

The hair cutting was not easy. The moon had moved and there was not much light, now. And a dagger is not a good barbering tool. Still, at last it was done, and Madoc held a heavy sheaf of black hair over his arm. Neva tossed her head, amazed at the lightness of it. She laughed.

"I could grow accustomed to this. Now there is just one more thing." She hesitated, because though she had made up her mind, it was hard to do. "I want you to take the ring, too."

"Your mother's ring! But, why?"

"Because it is clearly costly, and no one in Melyni's service would leave it behind. It will be further proof that I am dead. When you tell her it was my mother's betrothal ring, she will know that only in death would I have parted with it."

"Yes, that is a point."

"I think you must not see her yourself, though. Send them to her with a message. Give them to Agathe, and say that you have gone to dispose of my body, lest it be found by a peasant or someone who would recognize it. Then make all the haste you can to join Linet. You must not be taken before the queen. If she bespelled you once, she can do it again."

"Perhaps. At any rate, I have no wish to be questioned by her or some of her followers. I will take your advice, little Princess."

91

Before they parted he gave her his dagger. She did not think it would be of any use to her, but she saw that to refuse it would make him unhappy. She put it into her pack.

He advised her to find the river and follow it, as it ran west, but to stay among the trees where she could hide if anyone came along. She promised she would, and they went their separate ways.

She found the river easily, and made her way along the top of the bank for awhile. It was lighter here. The trees were near enough so she could glide in among them in need, but the bank itself was clear, so the going was easy. Her feet made so little sound on the moss that she surprised a family of otters, playing in the water. Now and then the river spread into a pool, and once she saw a raccoon there, fishing. The air was clean and sweet, and she felt the spirit of adventure rising again.

But she was growing very tired. She began to look around for a place to rest, and finally chose a tree to the left of the bank. It was large and had a little v-shaped opening at the base of its trunk. She was able to nestle into the opening, and with her dark cloak over her and the shadow of the branches wrapping her round she felt safe. She didn't intend to sleep, only to rest, but her long day, interrupted night, fright, and long walk had left her more tired than she had realized, and her eyes closed almost at once.

Chapter Nine
Sevenhills

Mossy ground and a tree trunk, no matter how cozy, do not make a comfortable bed when one is accustomed to soft down and velvet. When Neva woke it was still night, though the sky was turning from black to pale purple, and dawn could not be far away. She was very stiff and chilly. She got up, yawning, and made her way down to the river. It was wide and slow moving here, and she was able to splash water on her face and hands. She smoothed her hair, smiling at its shortness.

By the time she was ready to resume her journey the sky was flushing coral and gold. It was going to be a nice day.

It wasn't until she had walked for several minutes that she began to notice something strange about the woods. Last night, before she had gone to sleep, she had looked down the bank and seen that it was bare for a long way. But now there were many trees: willows, alder and aspen. They grew thickly, with underbrush between them, and they were larger than any trees she had ever seen before.

"Well," she murmured, "I'm getting farther into the woods, I suppose. I have never been so far. And I must have been wrong about the riverbank. It was so dark."

She was obliged to go around the trees, and then around others, so soon she wasn't going due west anymore. It was hard walking. There were roots knotting the forest floor, large and twisted ones. And though the sky above was blue, now, the trees were so big and so close together that it was dark. They didn't dance in the breeze in a friendly fashion but hung stiff, and holes or scars in the trunks seemed to glare down at her. The air was heavy.

But it wasn't until she came to a small open place that the true meaning came to her. There, rising in peaks and pinnacles against the sky were mountains. Mountains! So close! How could that be? From all she had heard she must still be miles from them. Why she wasn't even in the deep forest yet! She couldn't be!

But, looking around at the enormous trees, she knew that she was. This was no longer the bright, friendly wood, Rowan's wood. Somehow, by some magic, it had changed. Whose magic? Her stepmother's? But if Madoc had reached her and she believed Neva dead, why would she bother? And if Madoc had not yet reached her, she would hardly make it more difficult for him by moving the countryside around.

There were, of course, other workers of dark magic in the world, especially in the deep forest. There were witches and wizards, and perhaps even giants. And dragons. Dragons had great power. If word had gone out that someone was wandering alone and unprotected toward the mountains, Something could have worked magic to bring her closer. She swallowed and then tried to conjure up a more cheerful idea. Something good could have worked a white magic to shorten her journey, too. She thought of the unicorn and the naiad and the Lady of the Faerie. It was an encouraging idea – that the faerie queen might be watching over her.

She crossed the clearing and was in among the trees once more. She walked more slowly, picking her steps, noticing as she went that there were toadstools instead of flowers growing here and there, some of them almost as bright as flowers but poisonous and in odd shapes. The moss was nearly all gray, no longer green or gold. It was not a friendly forest, and she found herself shivering as she walked. She wasn't sure where she was. Far from the abbey, she thought; far even from the village that nestled in the foothills, and from which peddlers often came to Roldene. She was beyond both of them. The ground was rising, and she frequently had to stop to catch her breath. She must be climbing the foothills but she could not be sure. The forest was so thick that she could see nothing but trees.

She stopped only once that day, to eat a bit of lunch and drink some water. Her water would not last long, and she was worried about refilling her flask from the river. Though it was out of sight, she could tell by the sound that it was moving very fast now. It wouldn't be easy to get down to it, and when she did, the current might easily sweep the flask right out of her hand. *I must be more careful with the water, that's all*, she thought. *And maybe later the river will slow down. There might even be a pool somewhere.*

She was bitterly tired by late afternoon, and beginning to worry about the coming night. She would have to find shelter. She couldn't possibly sleep out in the deep forest, with wolves and wild cats and bears prowling about – not to mention worse things, such as manticores, gryphons and perhaps even - so near the mountains -- dragons. She had told Madoc that she would be protected against wild beasts, but now in this dark and fearsome forest she was not so sure.

There was a gleam of light ahead, a more open spot, and she moved toward it, thinking it would be good to stand in a clearing and see something besides trees on either side. When she got there she found that it was not only a clearing but a yard, and in the yard was a house, long and unusually low, hardly taller than a child's play cottage. It was beautifully built of stone, each one laid smoothly on the next, as if made by a master builder, and the thatch of the roof was woven into intricate patterns. The door was red and curved at the top, and the knob and key plate were of gold.

Neva stood still, gazing at it. It might be a witch's house. But they seldom built so well, unless of course they were building of gingerbread, sugar and the like to tempt unwary children. It was far too small to belong to a giant, and elves and other Good Folk did not dwell in houses that looked like houses. There was no smoke coming from the chimney, and the windows were shuttered. It was possible that no one lived there anymore. Or perhaps they were out for the day. Still, despite misgivings, she walked slowly to the door and knocked. There was no answer. She tried the knob but it was locked. Well, if she lived in the deep forest, she might lock her door, too – not that locks were very good at keeping out witches and such, but there were always unwelcome tramps. *Such as myself,* she thought, smiling wryly and beginning to turn away.

Yet somehow she didn't want to leave. There was a feeling about this low house – as if it were waiting for her, as if this was shelter and sanctuary. She could not understand why, but slowly she turned back. Automatically she reached up to touch the blue stone, and it was warm to the touch. The key beside it brushed her hand.

It will open doors for you if ever you need them opened.

The words were so clear she could almost hear Rowan's voice saying them.

She drew a deep breath and slipped the chain over her head. "All right, Rowan," she murmured and tried the key in the lock.

It had fit Rowan's cottage cupboard, and it fit this lock, too. It turned smoothly.

The door opened noiselessly on well-oiled hinges, and she stepped into a long hallway, with openings at the end, one on each side. All along the gleaming walls were doors with golden knobs. She hesitated and then called, "Is anyone home?"

There was no answer, so she closed the door behind her. At once the hallway was very dark, but when she made her way to the right-hand opening there was enough sunlight coming from between the shutters to show the room clearly. It was a sitting room, apparently, with sofas and easy chairs and one beautifully fashioned rocker. All the furniture was upholstered plainly in some dark material like corduroy, with no frills, yet the lamps on the carved tables were of silver, with raised figures decorating them, and the fireplace utensils were of gold. But the strangest thing was the size. Everything was child size.

It was as she was studying the lamp nearest her, and admiring the delicacy of the work, that she thought, *it looks dwarf-made*, and suddenly the answer came to her. It was a dwarf house!

That explained the size, the fine craftsmanship, the precious metals used for everyday things. It had to be!

Most dwarves chose to live in caverns created by themselves and made not only comfortable, but luxurious through their skill. But sometimes they built houses near the mountains where they worked. Rowan had spoken of the dwarf Redstol and his sons, one of whom was Thunel, the artist. They dwelt deep in the forest, she had said. Could this be their house?

She looked into the room that opened from the opposite side of the hall. It was a dining room, with a long, low table and seven chairs. They were of carved wood, as were the sideboard and china cabinet. This last had doors of clear glass, and inside she could see wooden and earthenware dishes, with some silver and gold pieces gleaming among them. And on the top shelf was a bread basket woven with silver, like her own basket. Thunel's work. This must truly be his home.

She went into the sitting room again and sank into an armchair with a weary sigh. She hoped Thunel was just out for the day, not off on a journey. She was sure he would not turn her away. And Rowan had spoken warmly of his father Redstol. If she could just rest here until morning, tomorrow, perhaps, they might tell her the best route through the mountains.

The chair she sat in was low but comfortable, and she was small enough to fit into it cozily, with her weary feet on the footstool. She thought about food but was too tired to open her pack. She closed her eyes, and drifted into sleep.

"What in the name of the One have we here?"

"A maiden, by Thor!"

"A trespasser!"

"How lovely she is!"

"But what has happened to her hair?"

"What do I care what has happened to her hair or how lovely she is? I want to know what she is doing here!"

"Need you always be so hotheaded, Flone? She is plainly harmless."

"How did she get in? The door was locked! I have suspicions about maidens with hair cut man-style who force their way into people's houses! Wake her up and make her explain herself, that's what I say!"

Neva was deep in a dream, and it was several minutes before the voices began to break into her sleep. When at last her eyes opened she couldn't think where she was. She had been dreaming about Rowan and her father, on a happy day when she was young and they three had spent a rare evening together.

She blinked in the firelight at the short, muscular figures around her, their bearded faces registering astonishment, curiosity, admiration, and intense annoyance, depending on where she looked. For a moment she thought she was still dreaming, and then reality came to her suddenly, as she remembered. Dwarves! She was in the home of dwarves, and they had returned and found her sleeping in their sitting room, without so much as a by-your-leave! No wonder they – well, one of them, anyway – looked annoyed!

"Oh," she said, struggling to her feet, "I beg your pardon, truly I do! I was so tired, and I felt so safe and comfortable that I fell asleep! Is - is this Thunel's home?"

"Are you a friend of Thunel's, child?" asked a dwarf with snowy hair and beard.

"Yes – that is, we met and spoke once, and he was a friend to me. I am Princess Neva of Verlain."

A murmur of surprise went around the circle. Now that she was properly awake she saw that there were six of them, all much alike except for the color of their hair, which was brownish red, brown, grey, silver streaked with black, or pure silver. The silver-haired one had more wrinkles on his face and was plainly the eldest.

"I am Redstol the Dwarf," he said. "Thunel is my son. He will be home soon. These are his brothers, Flone, Bolyn, Lode, Galt, and Revis."

Each bowed as he was introduced, but Flone was still scowling.

"How did you get in?" he asked.

"I have a key," said Neva. "Long ago my godmother Rowan gave it to me, and said it would open any door I needed to open. I - I suppose I thought because it worked that it was all right for me to enter, but I see now that I was very rude. Please forgive me."

But as if by magic all the faces cleared. "The Key!" exclaimed Flone. "The Lady Rowan's key! We made it at her request long ago! And she is your godmother? Then of course you are welcome here, Princess!" And he bowed again, this time a real bow.

"But – indeed you are welcome, goddaughter of Rowan – but what brings you here?" asked Revis. He spoke more gently than his brother, and it was he who had looked at her with such admiration.

"My stepmother wants to kill me," said Neva simply. "I am running for my life."

There were murmurs of dismay.

"Troubled as we were to hear of the marriage of your father to the dark princess, we hoped it would not come to this pass," said Redstol. "This is ill news, indeed. We must hear the whole story, but first let us eat. Are you hungry, Princess? You are welcome to such plain food as we have."

Neva said that she was hungry, and the meal that was presently laid upon the table in the dining room, though plain, turned out to be delicious. It was a rich stew of vegetables and meats, and with it there was bread of wheat and rye, butter, soft cheese, and golden ale. Neva drank only water, but she ate hungrily. She had never eaten stew before, and she thought it was the best thing she'd ever tasted.

As they ate she told them all her story. They listened, shaking their heads gravely.

"It is a grievous thing," said Redstol. "The princesses of Prayn have always had too much power and used it for their own greed and gratification. Vain they are, and proud. Kilse the Witch Queen wanted to see her daughter on the throne of Verlain, for your father's kingdom is the largest of the Southern Kingdoms, and when your father wed your mother instead, she was very angry. That anger she certainly passed on to her daughter. Not that it would be necessary: Melyni herself would never forgive an insult like being passed over, especially for a blacksmith's daughter."

Knowing Melyni as she now did, Neva could see that this was definitely true.

"Do you think she means harm to my father?" she asked worriedly.

"She has him in her power, and that is harm enough. But I feel certain that, knowing he loves you, it would please her to hurt him through you. I believe she meant from the beginning to destroy you in some way, both to strike at him and because you are your mother's daughter. It would perhaps have been a more subtle, slower plot if you had been less lovely and talented, and so enraged her in your own right. But all this is conjecture and really doesn't matter now. She has struck, and her stroke failed."

"This stroke failed," said Lode. "But she will soon learn that you live, and where you are."

"And she has allies in the mountains," said Flone. "You have no chance of reaching the High King on your own, Princess. It was a brave plan, but you cannot possibly carry it out."

"But what can I do, then?" Neva asked.

There was silence as they all considered it. As they sat in thought they heard the door open and a cheerful voice called, "Ho, brothers and Father Redstol! I am home and successful!"

They heard a thump, as of a heavy pack being lowered, and a moment later Thunel appeared in the doorway.

"Why – Princess Neva!" he exclaimed. "Child, how came you here? And what has happened to your hair?"

His father quickly told him the story. His face darkened as he listened.

"I have feared for you ever since the wedding," he said. "Indeed, it was my intention to visit Roldene this next week, and perhaps the castle, too (though the dark queen has little use for our family), to discover if I could how things were going with you. I am glad your steps led you to our door."

"We have told the princess that she must not think of trying to cross the mountains on her own," said his father.

"No, nor at all," said Thunel at once. "I have wandered through them and I know of what I speak. Even without your stepmother's ill-will following you, you could never do it. Let me go to the High King for you. You must stay here, safe with us."

"Thank you," Neva said. "I am truly grateful for the offer, but would I be safe, even here? If she discovers where I am, won't she simply send someone after me? And she would be angry at you for giving me sanctuary, and do some terrible thing to you all. But if you are willing, perhaps you could guide me through the mountains."

"We must think this over carefully," said Redstol. "It is late now, and all of us are weary. You shall stay here tonight, anyway, Princess Neva, and in the morning, before we go to our work, we shall have a council."

"Yes," said Galt, who had not spoken before. "We have some power of our own, but dwarf magic is not a match for the power of Prayn. We must consider carefully what is best to do."

"You shall have the room my daughter Coppile used before her marriage," said Redstol. "It is a dwarf maiden's chamber, not a princess's, but it is comfortable. Let us drink the night-cup and make ready for bed."

The night-cup was a strong, sweet drink, served in a large silver cup with two handles, and passed from one to another with wishes for a good night. As Revis passed it to Neva he said, "Drink, welcome guest, and sleep in peace and safety. Let your troubles fade away. We, of the house of King Braldor, nevertheless recognize the authority of the High King, and set ourselves against all enemies of his people, and all things of the dark. Whatever comes of our council tomorrow, we will defend you with our lives."

Neva saw them all nodding, and a great sense of peace rolled over her. Trust no humans, the naiad had said. But dwarves were not human. She could trust them. She was no longer alone.

The little bedchamber to which she was led was neat and comfortable, and the bed, though the sheets were of rough cotton, not silk, were smooth, and the mattress was soft. Her pillow smelled wonderful, like herbs. She stayed awake only long enough to murmur a prayer of thanks, and then she slept deeply and long.

The council took place after breakfast the next morning, in a large room at the back of the house. A graceful harp stood in one corner, and several other musical instruments stood on shelves around the room. On a raised dais was a great chair of oak, carved and polished, and below it were six other chairs in a semi-circle. The large one was for Redstol, the others for his six sons. A slender chair with embroidered cushions was brought for Neva and set next to Thunel's.

It was a long discussion. The dwarves were all agreed that a journey through the mountains, even guided and guarded, was too dangerous for Neva. They seemed to have power to defend themselves against the evil things dwelling there, and they were on good terms with all non-magical wild beasts, but they were not sure that they could defend her, even if two or three of them went with her. And the more there were, Galt pointed out, the more noticeable they would be, and the easier it would be for Melyni to find them.

Thunel did suggest that they take her through the mines but that was quickly voted down. They could not take a stranger that way without permission from their king, and getting that would take several days. Even though Redstol was the king's son, he seemed in great awe of his father. And from what Rowan had told her of the dwarves and their kingdom, Neva could understand why. The dwarf king had greater power than almost any other nonhuman leader. His kingdom was vast and immensely wealthy, for he had access to all the precious gems and minerals in the world. He was a figure to respect.

Revis, Galt, and (strangely) Flone agreed with Thunel's second suggestion that he go to the High King, and Neva stay here with the dwarves. They felt that Thunel had the best chance of getting through without mishap.

"Everything in the mountains knows him," said Galt. "They are used to seeing him traveling with his pack on his back, peddling his wares. Everyone knows that he is not like the rest of us. But the sight of one or two dwarves traveling toward the High Kingdom would arouse curiosity, if not worse."

"Moreover," said Flone, "none of the rest of us can leave our work. We are preparing gifts of tribute, which are given yearly to the king, and they must be finished by the day when the Metal Circle is joined. We are already behind."

"I will gladly go," said Thunel, "and we can put a circle of protection around Sevenhills, so that Princess Neva can be safe during the day, while you are at work."

Sevenhills was the name of their house and land, so called because it stood in a valley, surrounded by seven peaks, Revis explained.

"We can do so," said Redstol, "but the circle can be broken."

"Only if one inside invites the enemy in," said Flone.

"As far as we know," Lode said.

Bolyn, obviously the eldest of the sons, spoke slowly. "We have not asked the princess if she would like to stay. We are bachelors and dwarves; we live roughly, and do not have royal manners. And what would she do all day? Sitting unoccupied, waiting for the dark queen to strike, would break the nerve of a warrior, never mind a gently raised princess."

Neva looked around at their faces and saw that they considered this thought a breach of hospitality. Yet Bolyn had spoken courteously. He had not said, as he might have, "Why should we expect a princess, soft and spoiled, to be content with our way of living, and what will she do with herself?" He might even have felt some discomfort at having a bored maiden wandering around their home and poking through their belongings while they were away.

"I would go on this quest myself," she said, "but since you say it is hopeless, I will gladly accept your kind hospitality. Rowan taught me many skills not usually taught to princesses, and I will keep your home tidy and cook your meals in return. I know

106

something of gardening, too, and can tend Thunel's plants. And in the evening I will sing to you." She smiled, looking around at the instruments. "You must be fond of music."

A light sprang into Bolyn's eyes. "Sing? Do you sing?"

"Were you not listening last night, brother?" Revis asked. "It was partly because of her voice that the queen became jealous. And has Thunel not told us how the people call her the snow singer?"

"You will not have to labor hard for us, Princess," said Lode. "A friendly elf once gave us a magic pot which creates anything we wish to eat – although I do admit that after a time there is a certain sameness to the taste," he added, grinning, "and a few flavoring herbs would not be scorned."

"And you are welcome to use anything in my garden, and in my workroom," said Thunel. "And I will leave you my harp."

The thought of someone to sing to them seemed to have turned the balance in her favor as far as Bolyn was concerned. The others, she thought, had already made up their minds.

"We shall put it to a vote," said Redstol, "as the custom is. Shall Thunel go to the High King, and Princess Neva stay here with us?"

All seven raised their hands and said, "Yes!"

"Then," said their father, "as the princess is willing, we shall give her sanctuary while Thunel goes on the journey."

Thunel had just returned from a long trip, selling his wares, and would not normally have set off again so soon. He usually stayed home for some time, weaving and creating and tending his garden. But he assured Neva that he was not tired, that he had plenty of things with which to replenish his stock. He would go laden as usual, so not to arouse curiosity in anyone seeing him.

Redstol and his other five sons left directly after the council, to their work in the mines, and Thunel and Neva were alone. He showed her over the whole house, which had many rooms: bedrooms, workrooms, a treasury, and a storeroom where his mother, when she was alive, and his sister, before her marriage, used to keep stone crocks of preserved fruits and bottles of honey from the bees which they had tended. A long room at one end of the house was used for the dwarf king and his court on the rare occasions that they visited.

"When my grandmother was living, they came more often," said Thunel, "for Father Redstol was her favorite son. And she liked to pay visits. I think I got my wanderlust from her. The king prefers to stay in his own caverns and receive callers. He is fond of all his children, including Father Redstol, but he doesn't like to leave the mountain."

Lastly he showed her his garden. It was large and neatly divided by low stone stiles to separate the vegetables that liked each other from those that didn't (it was a surprise to Neva that some vegetable grew better if close to, or separated from, others). There was also an herb garden with wheels and beds, such as Rowan used, and a flower garden. There were benches for the dwarves to sit on and enjoy the grass and flowers.

"Dwarves have a reputation for caring nothing about flowers," said Thunel. He grinned. "But my brothers, except for

Flone and Lode, often sit out here. Flone and Lode would be embarrassed to be caught at it."

Late in the day, Thunel prepared his pack and departed.

"There is a spell on the house and gardens to keep out all evil things, as we told you," he said, "but we do not know whether or not the dark queen could break it. So take care, little snow singer. When the queen learns where you are, as she surely will, she will try to attack, and it may be in a way you do not expect."

Neva felt that this was true, and she promised to take care. She watched from the garden gate until he was out of sight and then returned to the house, feeling lonely and at a loss. Well, she had given her quest to someone else, and now she had naught to do but sit and wait, like a lady in a tale, for the hero or prince to come to her rescue. She never had cared for that kind of story or that kind of lady. And, she thought, pulling herself up short, she was not one of them. She would not sit sighing at her embroidery frame, wistfully watching the road for her deliverer. There was work to be done here – the house could use a good cleaning to begin with – and there was nothing weak and lazy about housekeeping. She would keep herself busy, and keep a watch out for an attack by her stepmother, and when Prince Liam did come riding up to the door (and it would be good to see him; she would not pretend otherwise) it would not be to rescue her, but to ride as her escort to his father's house.

Chapter Ten
Waiting

Even so she often thought, as the days went by, that she could not have borne the waiting if it had not been for the music. Every morning, after the dwarves had gone to their work, she would tidy their house, work for awhile in the garden, and then, returning to the house, she would take Thunel's harp and play and sing. An afternoon would pass quickly that way, and when the shadows grew long she would know that it was time to stop and make a meal. Sometimes she used the magic pot, sometimes she cooked things she remembered Rowan making long ago, but the dwarves were always grateful. One of them would wash the dishes afterwards, and the rest would gather in the council room for more music.

Neva taught them many songs, and they taught her some dwarf songs, which were hard to sing but rich and exciting to listen to. They were written for their deep male voices, and one day she asked a question she had often wondered about.

"Revis," she said (they were together, putting the instruments away after the others had gone to bed one night), "why are there no songs written for female dwarves? Don't they sing?"

"Indeed they do," he said, "but their music is not like ours. Ours holds the bones of the earth and the wealth of the mines and the joy of the hard labor in its notes. But theirs is made of the delight of creating beautiful things, the wisdom that holds the families and councils together (all our councilors are females), the love and grace and warmth of those who feel life itself grow within them. Also they have many dancing songs. When next I see my sister I will ask her if she will come and teach you some. They are seldom written down, for they spring from the heart."

The sons of Redstol spoke often of their sister. They missed her, and as Redstol himself said once, Neva's presence among them filled the empty space left in their household by her marriage.

So the days went by, and nothing was heard from the queen, and slowly Neva became less watchful. She was still quick to slip into the house if she saw a movement among the trees while she was in the garden, but she was not tense as she had been at first. Yet she often wondered uneasily why Melyni had done nothing. She must have discovered by now that Neva was alive, and where she was.

"Maybe as long as I stay away she is satisfied," she said to the dwarves one night.

"An envious heart is never satisfied," said Bolyn grimly.

Even if there had been no danger from Melyni, Neva would not have dared to wander away from the dwarves' house. The howling of wolves could sometimes be heard at night, and twice, as she worked in the garden, she saw a wildcat slink down the path. And once a shadow fell over her, and looking up she saw a gryphon – almost as rare now as dragons - flying overhead. There were tales of friendly gryphons but she would not want to risk meeting one. She hurried back into the house.

Then one afternoon a visitor came to the cottage.

Neva heard the knock as she was dusting in the far end of the house. She dropped her cloth and stood very still, her heart in her mouth.

"Thunel! Are you home? It is I, Kisa!" a young female voice called.

After a moment's hesitation, Neva moved into the front room and peered out a window. The caller was dressed like a country girl, and wore her straw-colored hair in rather untidy braids. She had a very plain but pleasant face, and she could not be more than fourteen. Anyone less like a servant of Melyni could hardly be imagined. This must be a customer for Thunel's wares.

The girl knocked again, and then glanced up and saw Neva at the window.

"Oh!" she exclaimed. "Who are you?"

She looked almost frightened and the last of Neva's doubts vanished.

"I'm the dwarves' housemaid at present," she said. "They are not home."

Kisa's face fell. "Oh! I was so hoping to find Thunel here. I brought some belts to trade for some of his rosewood wreaths. See!" She held up the prettiest belt Neva had ever seen. It was sky blue silk, embroidered with gold, and had a silver clasp.

"How lovely!" Neva exclaimed.

"It is, isn't it? My mother made this one. We weave them or cut them out of silk and embroider them. We even make some out of lace. Would you like to look at them?"

Neva yielded to temptation. "Wait," she said, "I'll open the door."

When the girl came in she looked around approvingly. "How neat and clean you keep this room," she said. "It was always so topsy turvy. Look, do you know when Thunel will be back? I could leave a few belts for him to look at."

"He left several days ago with things to sell," said Neva truthfully, "and I don't know when he will be back. But he has several wreaths made, and I don't think he would object if I exchanged them for such lovely belts. He could sell these, I am sure." She lifted one or two out of the open basket and looked at them admiringly.

"Oh, that would be wonderful. I would hate to have to tell Mother I had made the journey for nothing," said the girl. "Yes, he often sells our belts, especially when he goes to the bigger towns. And, look, I will give you this blue one for yourself. For saving me another trip back."

"Oh, but I couldn't take it! It's the most beautiful of all! It would bring a fine price!"

"But it was meant for you. The blue exactly matches your eyes. Look in the glass while I fasten it around you, and you will see."

There was a round mirror of precious glass hanging on the wall. Laughing a little, Neva turned to it as the girl clasped the belt around her waist. It fastened at the back, strangely enough. While Neva was thinking how strange this was, two other things happened. She realized, with a shock, that though she could see her own reflection clearly in the glass, there was no reflection of the girl behind her. And before she could react to this, Kisa pulled the belt tight, so tight that all Neva's breath went out in a gasp and she could not draw another. The clasp clicked shut. Everything swirled around her and she felt herself falling. Just before the blackness engulfed her she heard a high, screeching laugh and her stepmother's voice exulting, "And it will never come unclasped, not-so- beautiful one!!"

Chapter Eleven
The Apple

When they found her lying on the floor that night, they thought she was dead. She wasn't breathing at all, and her eyes stared sightlessly at the ceiling. In their rage and grief they did not notice the belt at first – they might never have noticed it, had it not been so beautiful. They were not in the habit of noticing details of dress. But Melyni had erred in making it so striking.

It was Redstol who saw it first.

"What is this?" he asked. "This does not belong to the princess."

"A magic talisman of the Queen?" Bolyn suggested. "Can we remove it?"

They found the clasp but it was closed with some magic. They could not undo it. But they were dwarves and craftsmen, not to be balked by any made metal. Sure, now, that it would not be made unopenable unless removing it would undo the magic, they brought tools and cut through the clasp. And as the deadly belt fell away from her, Neva drew a long breath. Awareness came back into her eyes.

At first she couldn't think why she was lying on the floor with the six dwarves around her, all of them looking grim. Then she remembered it all.

"Oh!" she exclaimed. "It was Melyni after all!"

She sat up and her eyes fell on the belt. She shivered.

"She tried again to kill me," she said.

"And nigh succeeded," said Flone gruffly. "Princess, princess, why did you let her in?"

"No," said Redstol. "Time enough to hear the story when she has rested and had a hot drink. Revis, will you brew her one of your good ones? Lode, Bolyn, go outside and check that no one is about. Lean on me, Princess, and I will get you to a comfortable seat."

Neva found that her knees were very shaky and she was glad to lean on the old dwarf as she made her way to the cushioned chair that they kept for her. Soon Revis was back, bearing a carven chalice. It gave off a delicious steam.

Lode and Bolyn came in to report no one around. They could not even find footprints, though since the ground was hard and dry, that was no great surprise.

As she sipped the drink Neva told them her story. They shook their heads.

"She is cunning," said Galt darkly. "The peasant girl Kisa does indeed trade goods with Thunel, and she looks as you have described her. So, even had one of us been here to guard you, we might have let her in. Once we had asked her in, our spells would be powerless against hers."

"She thinks I am dead," said Neva. "Perhaps this will be the end of it now."

"No," said Redstol. "She has only to look in her mirror. She is sure to do so this very night." He smiled at Neva rather weakly. "Even as pale as you are, and looking as if you need rest, you are fairer than the queen or anyone else. She will soon know – may already know – that this scheme, too, has failed."

"She will try again," said Flone. "That is as sure as a hammer is steel. Snow singer, you must not go outside anymore, even into the garden. You must keep the shutters closed. And you must open the door to no one, not even one of us. If she can appear as Kisa, she could appear as anyone. You must not risk it."

Neva agreed but her heart sank at the thought of long days without a glimpse of the world outside, doing her work and making her music by lantern light.

"It will not be long," said Revis, guessing her thoughts. "Thunel must surely have reached the King by now, and if I know His Majesty, he will act quickly."

"I am guessing that Prince Liam might act even more quickly," added Lode, grinning at Neva. "I have heard that he thinks very highly of you."

Neva smiled, but she was not sure. Although she had responded right away to the letter from the prince, concerning her father's betrothal, it had been a rather stiff, formal response. It was the only kind she could write, because her father had been with her at the time, advising her as to how one should reply to the son of the High King, and sometimes looking over her shoulder. She had meant to write another, more friendly letter, explaining the first one, but there had been no chance before the wedding. And then Melyni had arrived. Under her spell, Neva had scarcely given Prince Liam a thought.

She was sure he would come for her. She did not doubt that. But she wondered if he still thought of her as a friend.

That night, as she lay in bed, gazing at the dark rafters, she cupped the stone and the key in her hands and thought about Rowan and about the Lady of the Faerie, who had sent her the stone. She wondered, not for the first time, if the Lady had foreseen the darkness that would come into her life. Did the Lady know where Rowan was? The faerie were strange folk, so the stories said, and did not love or care as humans did, so maybe it didn't matter to her that Rowan had vanished. Yet she had sent Neva the stone, and it had saved her life.

"If ever I am free and happy again," whispered Neva, "I will seek out the faerie and all others with power, and try to find Rowan. This I vow in the name of the One Who Hears."

She fell asleep, still clutching the key and the stone.

The days that followed were very dreary. It rained, and what little light that crept between the cracks of the closed shutters was grey and dull. Even with a fire on the hearth, the dwarves' house was chilly. They did not seem to feel it, accustomed as they were to the cold mines, but Neva felt as though she would never be warm again. Depression, new to her, rested heavily upon her. Not even music cheered her for long.

When the rain finally stopped it was better. And Revis sprained his wrist in the mines and had to stay home for a few days, so they were able to open the shutters and even the doors, and let the sun flood the rooms. It was wonderful to have company. They roasted apples and drank cider and told stories.

"I love apples," Neva told him. "When I was a very little girl my father would reward the person who could bring apples for me during the seasons when they were scarce. There was one kind – I never knew what they were called, but they were small and bright red, so shiny I could see my face in them. They had a sweet, tingly taste. Maybe they grew in the woods, because Rowan often found them for me, and sometimes Madoc the Forester brought some."

"I know the ones you mean," Revis said. "Ruby-fruit apples. They are unusual because they ripen very early. Summer apples, they are sometimes called, though it is May when they are at their best. Two miles from here lives an old woman who raises fruits and vegetables, and she has a ruby-fruit apple tree near her cottage. We often buy them from her."

Although Thunel grew some vegetables, it was not the main purpose of his garden, and the dwarves, said Revis, bought some of their food from the old lady, or from the village higher up in the mountains. Marketing was Thunel's chore.

"If he is not back soon, someone else will soon have to do it. And I predict that it will be I," he added, grinning. "I am the youngest. Also I am a dreamer and slow at my work, so I often get sent on errands when the others cannot be spared. I don't mind. It is a change from the mines."

Revis predicted rightly. A few evenings later Redstol said, "We are running out of apples and vegetables. Also cider! You two stay-at-homes have drunk almost all of it."

Revis and Neva exchanged a guilty smile. Neva had never tasted cider before she came to the dwarves' house, and she had fallen in love with the spicy, sweet taste. She had drunk more than her share.

"You will have to go marketing, Revis, as Thunel is not here," his father added. "Your wrist is still weak, so you will not be able to work much, anyhow. Try old Lumet first. She usually has all we need. That way you will not be gone long."

"She is the one with the ruby-fruit apples," Revis told Neva. "I will bring you some."

The next morning, as Neva watched Revis set off on his marketing journey she felt very lonely. To cheer herself up she sat down at the harp, and began idly to run her fingers across the strings. She found herself singing one of the songs that had been so warmly received at her twelfth birthday party. How long ago it seemed! She would be fifteen on her next birthday; it had not even been three years yet, but it seemed half a lifetime. She remembered that Countess Daril had been fifteen at that long ago party, and how grownup Neva had thought her.

Had Linet ever reached the countess? Had Daril sent word to the high king? Perhaps not. Perhaps she would rather not become involved. Why should she pit herself against Melyni?

It was even possible that the High King would rather not interfere. After all, it was not as if the people of Verlain were suffering. What was the life of one young princess compared to the danger of unleashing Melyni's dark powers against the high throne?

Then she shook her head, tossing off the dark thought. No. Not if everything she had ever heard about the king was true. It was said he would risk his own life to save even the youngest peasant child from abuse. He would help her. She must not give way to despair.

She got up and began to plan a special meal to welcome the dwarves home tonight. They would be late because today they must finish their gifts to their king. Tomorrow was the meeting of the Metal Circle in the great caverns of which Thunel had told her. Revis would go, too. She would be alone for a day and a night. She knew that they were concerned about this, but it could not be helped. No excuse, short of death, was accepted for not attending this important meeting.

Revis returned with a basket full of vegetables but none of the lovely ruby-fruit apples.

"She has not yet gathered them," he said, "but she has given me her leave to go and pick some myself. I will go after the Metal Circle Meeting. We have a week of holiday, so several of us could go, and then it would be safe, surely, for you to come with us. Would you like that?"

"Oh, yes! I am so very tired of being inside!"

"I told Lumet about you. That is, I told her that we had a guest who was fond of ruby-fruit apples. I did not tell her who you were, though I doubt if she knows one king's daughter from another. She seldom goes farther from home than to the village market once a year, and she is interested in nothing but her garden."

When the dwarves returned that evening they had not only the gifts for their king, but also something for Neva. They had made her a belt of gold set with rubies, and with a clasp shaped like a bird.

"Since you love pretty belts," said Lode. "This one has all our good wishes worked into it, to take away the memory of the evil magic of the one from the queen."

Neva was delighted and moved, and she felt ashamed of her depression of the morning.

She had made carrot soup and small flat scones, and for a special treat an apple tart. After eating they sat up long, singing and telling stories. It was a merry evening, and she went to bed full of happiness. This was a good life, she thought. If only there were no threat from the queen she could be happy here forever.

In the morning, before the dwarves left, Redstol gave her some good news.

"A message has come from Thunel. He has arrived at the royal house, and by now will have seen the High King. There was also a messenger there from the Countess Daril. The countess was so disturbed by what has happened to you that she herself was on her way to see the High King, and may now have arrived. I think things will soon begin to happen."

"That makes me think," said Revis thoughtfully. "Yesterday, on my way back from Lumet's cottage, I met Alyn the Gnome. He had come from the east, and told me that Queen Melyni had gone, with many of her household, to Prayn. I thought at the time that it was ill news. Why should she go, except to be in touch with more magic than she could find in her husband's home? But now it occurs to me that she may be putting up barriers to protect herself against the vengeance of the High King. If so, she may be too busy looking after herself to plan any more attacks against Neva."

"That may be so," said his father, "or it may not. But do not relax your guard, Princess. If she does strike, it will be in a different way from before, of that I am sure. In a way we least expect."

Neva was sure of that, too. As she watched the dwarves marching away toward the mountains she felt lonely and scared. It would be a long two days.

She barred the door and closed the shutters. Then she opened one of them again. She could not stand to spend all that time in the dark. She would stay away from the window, and nothing could induce her to open the door to anyone.

As she tidied the cottage she thought about the High King and wondered if he would truly turn his forces against Melyni. She had not expected that. She had hoped that he would somehow protect her, perhaps bring her to his palace, as the prince had twice suggested. But to attack the dark house of Prayn ... She knew, now, how powerful that house had always been. The dwarves had told her all (and more) than she wanted to know about the witch-queens. Could anything stand against that evil?

She heard footsteps outside and froze where she stood. Then Revis's voice, rather breathless, called, "It is only I, Princess. Don't stop what you are doing. I only want to say that we met old Lumet on our way to the mines, and she has harvested her apples and will bring a basketful later today. I said no one was home. She will leave them by the garden door; it should be safe enough for you to bring them in after she is gone. Take care, and we will be back the day after tomorrow."

Then his steps pounded away again.

Neva smiled. How like Revis to bring her the message, at risk of being late for his meeting, so that she would not be frightened when she heard the old woman outside the door! He had a kind heart. How lucky she had been to find the dwarves' house that day!

123

If she ever had it in her power she would like to do something wonderful for them, though truly there was little that they needed. They were content with their lives as they were.

It was several hours later that she heard the garden gate click, and lighter but slower footsteps approach the door. She looked up from the shirt she was mending for Redstol and saw through the window a bent old woman in a faded cloak with a basket of glowing apples. She set it down and turned away without even glancing at the house. Neva saw her move out of sight and heard the gate click behind her.

Neva finished the shirt before rising and going to bring in the apples. She looked carefully out the window first but no one and nothing was in sight, not so much as a robin or a rabbit. She opened the door just wide enough to pull the basket in, then shut and bolted it once more. Then she carried the basket into the pantry.

The apples looked lovely, deep red and shining. They were too good to cook with: small, perfect eating apples. The one on top was truly almost the shade of the ruby for which it was named. It was perfectly round, and not a blemish showed on its satin skin. She picked it up, unable to resist, and held it in her hands for a moment before biting into it.

It was delicious, sweeter than she remembered any apple being, yet with a nutty flavor to the coolness. She ate it greedily, like a child with a sweetmeat, and considered another.

Later she would recall bending forward to pick up another, but that was all she remembered. There was a sudden roaring in her head, a moment of dizziness, and darkness engulfed her as she struck the floor with a crash. The core of the poisoned fruit fell from her lifeless hand.

Chapter Twelve
Vision: King Verl

In the great bed in the high chamber of the royal castle of Verlain, King Verl lay in slumber. He was dreaming. Strange dreams. Disturbing dreams. He saw his daughter running down a path, pursued by great bats with wingspans miles wide which cast shadows over the world. They were gaining on her.

"Run! Run!" he wanted to cry, but he could make no sound. He could not move, either, he could only watch in terror as they swooped down upon her.

Watching in anguish and fear he struggled to go to her aid, aware of a cold feeling that somehow he himself had put her in this danger. He saw her fall and the bats came down, blocking her from his view, and in his anguish he cried aloud, "Neva! Neva!" The sound of his own voice awakened him, and he lay, icy cold and shaking, looking around the room wildly.

A dream, he thought. Only a dream.

But the dread was still upon him and he wanted to get up, and go to her room to make sure she was all right. He had not seen her for a long time. How long? And why not? The questions came into his fuzzy mind with surprising force and clarity. He could not remember seeing her since long before the day of the picnic at the river palace, yet somehow he had never noticed it. How could that be?

126

"Witchcraft," said a soft voice, and he sat up quickly. Whose voice was that? He knew it, and yet...

"Rowan?" he asked, looking around the empty chamber.

"I cannot come to you, dear king," the voice said. "I have not the power. But you can hear me, so the spell must be weakening. Listen to me. You married the Princess Melyni, and she has darkened your mind with poisons and witchcraft. Your daughter was forced to flee for her life. She is in deadly peril, and her life hangs on a thread. Now, while your wife is away in her mother's castle, preparing to defend herself against the vengeance of the High King, you must act. The woodsman Madoc and his wife Linet are on their way to meet you. Tell Madoc to take you straight to the home of the seven dwarves who dwell in the foothills of the mountains. Let nothing and no one hinder you. Go today."

"Yes," said Verl, and for the first time in months his mind cleared and he felt wide awake and strong. "But where are you, Rowan?"

There was no answer. She was gone, if indeed she had ever been there at all.

The king rose and rang for his servants.

Chapter Thirteen
Sleep

There was no doubt in their minds this time. She lay as white as marble, not breathing, icy cold. No belt or other implement of magic was upon her, and she was dead.

They had carried her to her little bed when they found her, and now they stood around her, some weeping, some cold with rage, despair clutching them. They did not know what to do.

"Her father must be told," said Redstol thickly at last.

"Yes," said Lode. "Even if he is under the queen's spell, he must know what happened."

"I will go," said Revis. He stood with his fists clenched at his sides. His face was drawn and grey. "I will tell him what his queen has done. Yes, even if I die for it!"

They looked at him in surprise, for he was considered the least bold of them.

"She was like a sister to me," he said, answering their look. "I will have vengeance!"

"She was like a sister to us all," said Bolyn in his calm way, "and vengeance will come, but not now. Now is the time for grief. King Verl is not to blame for any of this. He is bewitched. Whoever goes, must go to carry him the news of his daughter's death, no more. Not blame or anger. And if we *are* to have vengeance, it might be well if the queen does not know we suspect her hand in this evil deed."

"Bolyn is right," said Redstol. "I myself shall go, a father to a father. The rest of you will make her a resting place."

He left in that same hour, and four of his sons went to their workshop, where they fashioned a casket out of pure gold. Revis stayed at the side of the princess.

"I know she is dead," he said when his brothers returned, "yet I do not believe it. I cannot bear to believe it, perhaps, and yet..."

They all looked at her. She was still lovely, and except for the fact that she was not breathing she could have been asleep.

"Who knows?" said Lode at last. "Perhaps she isn't. Perhaps this is witchcraft that makes her appear lifeless."

"And perhaps we are all fools," said Flone. "But I agree with Revis. My heart cannot accept it."

Galt, who seldom spoke, said, "I cannot bear to shut her away. We will lay in her the casket but we will not cover it. We will set it in the garden and take turns watching over it."

"Yes," said Bolyn. "At least – until – unless – there is some change in her."

So they built a raised stand and placed the golden coffin upon it. On the side in silver they engraved the simple statement, "Neva: A King's Daughter."

And they waited.

Chapter Fourteen
Vision: Prince Liam

Liam, Prince of the Royal House of Lyrlim, turned over painfully in his camp cot, and stared up at the deep blue ceiling of his pavilion. It was long past the mid of the night but he could not sleep. Partly it was the deep gash in his arm, where the dragon's claw had slashed him, and the burn on his shoulder from its fire. But he had been lucky. Many a knight or prince had come from a dragon fight with worse than that. He ought to be pleased with himself that he had been able to kill the beast so quickly. But he wasn't. He disliked killing anything, even a dragon who was threatening an entire village. Especially as he now suspected that the lord mayor of the town had lured the beast in, with his own daughter as bait, hoping to get the girl a prince for a husband. He had been very insulted and disappointed when Liam delicately explained that, though the Lady Wylla was indeed lovely, he could not marry her.

Perhaps, he thought, *if I had told them that my heart is given ... But how could I? I have not seen Neva since she was a child. I do not know how she feels. I must see her face to face before I can really know if she remembers me as I remember her.*

Yes, and that was really what was keeping him awake. Tomorrow he was riding to the castle of Verlain to see Neva. He had been worried about her ever since Verl of Verlain had married Melyni of Prayn; worried enough to write her twice. She had responded so coldly to the first, and the second she had not answered at all. He had no way of knowing if she had even got it, and that troubled him. Of course it had been long since they had seen each other. It must truly feel long to her, for the years between twelve and fifteen are years of great change. But he was sure that she would have answered if she could.

He had been setting off to ride to Verlain when the messenger came from the mountain village, begging for help against the dragon. No prince could ignore such a plea. But now his duty was done and he was going to see Neva. He wondered if she had changed very much, except of course to grow up. He didn't remember her face all that well, only that she was very pretty. But he remembered her voice. How it had haunted his dreams over the years! Such a voice!

Would she be glad to see him? Would her stepmother make things difficult? He wore a ring that had been in his mother's family for centuries, which was supposed to defend him against evil spells. He wondered if he would need it.

"You would have needed it, indeed."

The voice seemed to come from the air above him. He sat up, startled, looking around.

'Be at peace, Prince Liam," said the voice. "I am Rowan, godmother to Princess Neva, but I cannot come to you in person. Not yet. Listen. Neva was forced to flee her father's house, knowing that her stepmother meant to kill her. She found refuge in these mountains with the dwarf Redstol and his sons, one of whom went to your father with word of her peril. Even now the High King rides with all his white force against Melyni. But it was too late, and she had already struck with dark force against Neva."

He wondered for a moment if he was dreaming. But somehow he knew that he was not. Everyone knew about Rowan, Neva's godmother, said to be descended from the faerie. He felt chilled to the heart.

"No," the voice continued, "you need not fear yet. I said too late for your father, but perhaps not for you. You must ride at once to the house of the dwarves. There you will find Neva. I cannot tell you how to deliver her. That you must discover for yourself. But I will tell you that it can be done."

"Where do the dwarves live?" Liam asked. "How will I find the right ones? These mountains are full of dwarves."

"Thunel, son of Redstol, is even now approaching your camp. He will guide you."

The voice grew very faint, yet it seemed to be closer. He felt a warmth, like sunlight, rest on him briefly, and then it was gone, leaving only a trace of fragrance that reminded him of Neva's garden. And he realized that his dragon wounds had been healed and he was rested and full of energy.

He sprang from his cot, calling to his squire.

Chapter Fifteen
Awakening

King Verl, accompanied only by a page, Madoc the Woodsman, his wife Linet, and Redstol the Dwarf were the first to reach Sevenhills. Redstol had met the king's group early the next morning and had told them his news. The king refused to believe that his daughter was dead. He felt certain that Rowan would have come to him again if it was too late.

"And in any case, I must see her," he said, struggling to keep his voice steady. "We will go on."

But it was a silent and grief-stricken group that rode up to the dwarves' cottage at last. Linet had wept silently the whole time. Madoc blamed himself for not staying with the princess, to guard her or die with her, if need be. The little page, who had known Neva all his life, fought back tears, telling himself that the king's own attendant must be strong.

Flone and Revis were standing guard at the golden casket. They stepped back as their father led the little group into the garden. Revis turned his eyes away from the drawn face of the king as he looked down at the motionless form against the crimson cushions that lined the coffin. Linet gave a loud cry of grief.

"Oh, my lady! My lovely mistress!"

She sank to her knees and began to weep, but all the others stood silently, gazing down at the pale face, lifeless yet unchanged.

"She is not dead," said Redstol after a long silence. Bewilderment and wonder struggled in his voice. "It has been two days, and she is unchanged. She is not dead!"

Linet stopped sobbing. She sprang to her feet and looked again at her mistress. Then she looked at her husband.

"She is asleep," said Madoc doubtfully. "And yet..."

"It is not sleep as we know it," said the king at last. "She is not breathing."

"And she is cold. But we do not believe she is dead," said Flone.

"There is a story of a princess who slept for a hundred years," said the page timidly.

"There are many stories of many kinds of spells," Revis said impatiently, "but who knows the truth of any of them? And what difference does it make? If she is alive, still she is lost to us. We do not know how to break the spell."

"A spell," the king murmured.

He turned and made his way unsteadily to a bench beside Thunel's herb wheel. He sat down heavily.

"May the One forgive me," he said. "I brought this upon her. I was afraid when first I found myself in the Dark Castle, after the battle with the giants, but Melyni spoke so sweetly and cared for my wounds with her own hands, and I began to trust her. To -- to like her. Then, the night before I left, she gave me wine to drink, a kind I had never before tasted. And from that moment I could not forget her. And it is my little Neva who must pay for my folly."

"Do not blame yourself, Your Grace," said Madoc heavily. "You were enthralled. It would take a magician to resist the spells of the Dark House of Prayn. A great lord of magic, such as His Majesty the High King."

The other dwarves had come out.

"The High King is riding even now against the castle of Prayn," said Lode. "A message came from our brother Thunel. He himself wanted to accompany the king but was sent back. He should be here in another day, perhaps sooner."

King Verl looked at the knot of small men, stood up, and bowed.

"I have not even thanked you for caring for my daughter," he said. "May I know your names?"

Redstol had just finished introducing his five sons when the page exclaimed, "My lord king! Look! An army approaches!"

Then they were all aware of the sound of many horses, which they had been hearing without noticing it for some time. They turned to the road just as two knights in armor emerged from the forest, followed by a pony and some other riders.

"Not quite an army," said Madoc.

"Nay!" said Redstol, as the pony surged ahead. "It is Thunel!"

"And the young prince!" exclaimed Linet. "I remember his face well. It is Liam, son of the High King!"

Thunel sprang from his pony and opened the gate for the other riders.

"Welcome to Sevenhills, Your Highness," he said.

Then he turned to the others.

"Father," he said, "I bring Prince Liam, the son of the High King."

There was a flurry of greetings and bows and welcomes, but Liam brushed them aside. He dismounted and said, "Where is she?"

"The prince had a message about Princess Neva," said Thunel. "Is she here?"

Then, following the gaze of his brothers, he saw the coffin on the pedestal. Horror and grief wrenched his face.

"No!" he cried.

He ran to the pedestal. The prince followed him.

King Verl stood up and walked heavily over to stand by the seventh dwarf.

"She is bespelled," he said. "She is not dead."

"No," said Liam. "She is not dead. Rowan said she was not. But – what has happened to her?"

He was shaken. He did not know what he had expected but it was not this – Neva lying so still against the cushions of a golden casket. So still. So cold. So lifeless. So beautiful. He would have known her anywhere. She had the look of the twelve-year-old princess he had last seen, only older, as he had known she would be. The longer he looked at her, the less lifeless she appeared to him. True, there was no movement of breath under the blue-laced bodice. When he touched her hand it was cold. But she had some color still in her cheeks and she did not wear the look he had seen before on the dead – as if all earthly things were done for them. No. Rowan was right. He could waken her.

He bent and kissed her. If all the legends were true, perhaps...

Nothing happened. He took her hands in his.

"Neva!" he called. "Neva, awake! It is I, Liam! I have come for you!"

Nothing. And yet...

Something was different. Around her neck was a fine chain, with a blue stone and a silver key hanging from them. They had not been there before he kissed her, or they had been invisible. Looking at them he felt a quiver, the same kind he remembered feeling in the presence of certain things of power that his father had. He lifted them from her chest, then drew the chain carefully over her head. The key brushed against his own ring, the one he wore to protect himself from spells.

There was a flash of brilliant light, and a sound of far-off music. For a moment everything blurred before him in a mist of color. He heard his men and the dwarves and those other people crying out, and then it was over. He blinked. Neva lay as she had been before, except that the chain with the key and the stone were back around her neck.

"Well done, my prince," said a warm voice. "Or let us say, half done."

He whirled and found himself looking at a tall, dark-eyed woman dressed like a peasant, but somehow not looking at all like one.

"Rowan!" "Lady Rowan!" "My Lady!"

The cries came all at once, and she smiled around at all of them.

137

"Yes," she said. "I am back. King Verl, it is good to see you. Madoc, blame yourself for nothing. Linet, dry your eyes. All is not lost."

It was the first Liam had realized that the white-haired man, to whom he had barely given a glance, was Neva's father.

"King Verl!" he exclaimed. "Forgive me for not greeting you, sir! I did not realize! How came you here? The queen..."

"Is in her castle of Prayn, hopefully finding your father's forces more than she can handle. I am free of her, thanks to Rowan."

"All our stories can wait," said Rowan. "We must awaken our princess. Liam has done several things, all but one. And for that he is going to need the help of all of you. And especially you, King Verl. For you are her father."

They looked at Neva, who lay as she had before, then at each other.

"But what must we do?" Liam asked.

"That I cannot tell you," said Rowan gently. "Gather round her, all of you. Now think. *Why* do you each want to wake her?"

"She is like a daughter to me, and a sister to my sons," said Redstol.

"She is my mistress," said Linet. "I have served her all her life."

"And I," said Madoc. "What do you mean, Rowan? You know why we want to awaken her! We all love her. Except, perhaps, for the prince."

"I, too, love her," said Liam quietly, and he took Neva's hands in his again.

"And you, King Verl?" said Rowan.

"She is my child. The daughter of my lovely Varena. I love her more than my life."

"We all love you, Neva," Liam whispered. "Please wake up."

The lashes against the marble face were very long and black. They moved. The hands he held felt warmer. He caught his breath. He bent and kissed her once more.

Her eyes flew open. They stared up at him in amazement and confusion.

"Prince Liam?" she asked. "But – what – where am I? What is happening?"

Amid the great shout of joy that went up Liam lifted her out of her coffin and set her on her feet before her father and Rowan. Color flushed her cheeks and lips, and tears welled up in her eyes.

"Rowan! Father!" she cried, and flung herself into Rowan's arms.

The next few moments were a confusion of laughing, crying, questions half finished, answers half finished. The dwarves joined hands and danced around the garden, singing in their deep voices, and the prince's knights, who only half understood what was going on, drew their swords and waved them in the air in the sign of victory. Madoc and Linet embraced, and Rowan passed the restored princess to her father, then to Liam. He took her hand, and she dropped him a graceful curtsey.

"I don't know what happened," she said, "but I think you saved my life."

139

"I am not entirely sure what happened myself," he admitted. "You were enchanted, and now you are awake, and I..." He paused, not knowing how to tell her that if she had not awakened, his life would have been empty and savorless. "I feel as if the sun has come out," he said finally.

The dwarves ended their dance and gathered round.

"Your Grace, Your Highness, Princess Neva and noble friends," said Redstol, bowing, "may I offer you the poor hospitality of my home? We will drink the cup of gladness, kept in our family for only the most special occasions, and hear each other's stories. And the princess looks pale yet, she should rest."

"Yes," said Rowan. "Enchantments are not cast aside in a moment. I, too, would rest."

So everyone gathered in the music room of the dwarves' house. Redstol brought out a golden cup, engraved with such delicacy that only dwarves could have fashioned it, and passed it around. The drink was cool and sweet and spicy, and it lifted the heart with one sip.

Neva told them about the apple. Bending to pick up another one was the last thing she remembered.

"But how did the queen contrive to insert her spells into old Lumet's apples?" Revis wondered. "Lumet is a good soul, and honest. She would never agree to being part of an evil scheme."

"She did not," said Rowan. "It was not Lumet you met on the way to the mine that morning, my friends, but the queen disguised to look like Lumet. Now you see how Neva was taken in the first time. Melyni is a mistress of disguise."

"Rowan, dear old friend," said the king, "it is your story I most want to hear. All else is becoming clear to me, but I would know where you have been all these years. Is it true that Melyni was able to bespell you? Even you?"

"Even I," said Rowan. "It was my own lack of caution that was my downfall. Or perhaps my wish to do more than I had originally set out to do. When first I learned that you, King Verl, had been carried wounded to the dark castle I at once suspected some evil. Although Melyni had taken great pains to assure everyone that she had forsworn the dark magic of her mother and grandmother and great-grandmother, I did not believe it. If that were so, she would have released the captives she held under her power."

"Captives?" the king asked.

"Not human captives. People of the Old Blood; beings of the elements. The family of Prayn had always had the power to entrap them. The Witch-Queen Kilse herself had enslaved at least two of them, and one was my old friend Cassin, a dryad with the gift of seeing the truth through lies and deceptions. Behind glass she held him and forced him to answer whatever question she cared to ask, whether weighty or trivial."

"The mirror!" Neva exclaimed. "It was your friend held there!"

"Yes. The mirror which Melyni used for her own pride and vanity."

"What mirror do you mean?" the king asked.

"It hangs in her private room, and she used to ask it daily who was the most beautiful woman in the world. As long as it assured her that she was, she was satisfied, but the day came that

141

Neva was more lovely, to Cassin's eye. He could not lie. He could not refuse to answer. Thus Melyni's jealousy, which was already smoldering over the matter of Neva's lovely voice, exploded into hatred, and she bent all her mind to destroying her."

"She would have committed murder because a young girl was fairer than she?" the king exclaimed.

"I wonder if it was that alone," said the prince. "She and her mother were both angry when you married Neva's mother, so I have heard."

"Yes," said Rowan. "They had planned to acquire the kingdom of Verlain to add to their power by having you marry Melyni, long before you ever met Varena. And they were angry when you chose the blacksmith's daughter over the dark princess. So Melyni would have no love for Varena's daughter to begin with. Still, had Neva been plain and untalented, she would have borne with her, got her married off as soon as possible, and forgotten her."

"So when you arrived at the dark castle to protect the king against Melyni you thought you might also set your friend free from the mirror?" asked Prince Liam.

"It was in the back of my mind. I did not go forth entirely heedlessly, however. I cast certain spells that might help Neva, should ill befall both her father and me. But I will talk of them later. I got to Prayn on the morning after Verl was wounded, and I immediately made my first mistake. I underestimated Melyni. I thought I could come and go without her knowledge, in the way I have. But she sensed my coming, and hardly had I materialized in the king's room then she also was there."

"I remember that," said King Verl. "I thought she greeted you with much courtesy."

"And so she did. She was extremely pleasant, and invited me to share her evening meal. But I could see into her mind. She was alarmed and angry. I assured her that I had come only so that I could bring back word to Verlain that their king was all right, and I thought I had convinced her, for her anger vanished, if not her alarm. But she insisted that I stay at least for the night, and that invitation I rashly accepted. It was my thought to see something of the dark castle while I was there, and perhaps free Cassin. If I could, the two of us would remove the king to a safer place. I alone could not do that. Again I underestimated her. I did not believe that she could read my thoughts, as I had read hers. Perhaps she could not, perhaps she only distrusted me, as well she might. However it was, that night as I slept she cast over me the same kind of spell that held Cassin and the others."

"She imprisoned you in glass?" Redstol asked, appalled.

"No, in a musical instrument. A harp."

"The harp!" Neva exclaimed.

"Yes. She thought, perhaps, that it would be amusing to have me compelled to answer to her touch as she played. But still she left me one ray of hope of eventual freedom. A very, very small ray and yet — Perhaps not. For there was a bond between Melyni and Neva which she could not know. They are both singers. And I had left behind me in my cottage a piece of music that might possibly break the spell. I had left it for Neva. She had a key that would open the cupboard where it lay. *If* she came to my cottage looking for me, *if* she opened the cupboard, *if* she took the music, *if* she sang it at the right place, in the right time, then possibly I could be freed."

"It doesn't sound like much of a chance to me," said Liam.

"No, it does not," said Rowan. "Yet it happened."

"I found the music," said Neva. "I was sure that you had left it for me, and I learned it. And the day Melyni tried to poison me, the day I ran away, I saw her secret room and the harp in it, and I felt somehow that I must sing the song. And I felt as if something happened when I did. But you did not appear."

"No. There are rules to spells and all things of power, one of which is the rule of three. Had you sung it thrice you would have released every captive thing in that room."

"And I didn't know!" Neva exclaimed. "I felt as if there were something more I should do, something I was overlooking, but I didn't know what."

"How should you? It was wonder enough that you sang it at all. And I was enough released from the twice-sung melody, to be able to pass out of the harp and into the stone which the Lady of the Faerie had made long ago for your protection. How much of this she had foreseen, I do not know. Nor how much of her power guided you to do what you did. Certainly that you overcame all those *ifs* was more than chance. Indeed, there is no such thing as chance, all things are part of a pattern."

"But Lady Rowan," said Flone, "if you were with Neva as she fled her father's house, and all through what followed, how was the queen able to attack her?"

144

"I was with her," said Rowan, "but I was still a captive. I could keep off direct danger, such as someone attacking her with a weapon, or even the threat of wild beasts. I made Madoc glance to Queen Varena's ring when, in his bespelled madness, he would have killed her. The enchanted belt was an outer thing, and my presence counteracted it, so that you were able to revive her. But I could not keep her from eating the apple, and once the poison entered her body, I could do nothing to stop it."

"Yet I didn't die," Neva said.

"The poison of the apple was not a poison that kills, whatever Melyni may have intended. It was a freezing spell from which only love could awaken you. And not only the love of your prince here." Rowan smiled at Liam and at Neva, and Neva blushed and dropped her eyes. "The love of your friends and the love of your father – most of all that, I think, for he too had escaped Melyni's spells – these were more powerful than the hate in the enchantment."

The cup went around again while they all silently thought over their respective stories and put together the pieces.

"But," said King Verl after awhile, "if you were imprisoned in Neva's stone, how were you able to appear to me?"

"And me," Liam added.

Rowan shook her head and smiled. "That is something I cannot explain. You might say you both dreamed me, you might say it was the power of Neva's need that enabled me to reach out to you, you might say it was part of the gifts of my family, and all those things would be correct. But they are not the complete answer. Nor can I explain how the power of Prince Liam's ring, touching the faerie stone, was able to set me free. The ring was a gift from the Lady of the Faerie to his family long ago, and the stone was a gift from her to Neva, but no one can explain how they work, not even the Lady herself. No one except the One."

"Then let us not ask," said Neva. "It is enough that I am awake and you are free. Let us give thanks for that."

She stood up, feeling strong and well again, and picked up the Thunel's small harp. Running her fingers across the strings she began to sing the song of thanksgiving that the churches of the southern kingdoms often sang. At first they listened, breathless, to the sweetness of her voice, and then they all joined in.

Liam sang with his eyes fastened on her lovely face, and she answered his gaze steadily with her own. And he knew that she knew what was in his heart. Later they would be alone, and he would tell her, and they would talk about a wedding day. But for now it was enough to blend his voice and his gaze with hers, and to give thanks.

Epilogue: by Rowan

The princess was delivered but it was not all over by any means. There was still the great battle at Prayn, where the High King, using the ancient powers born into his family, and the gifts given him by the Faerie, fought against the ancestral witchcraft of Queen Melyni.

That evening I approached Liam and Neva, who stood in the garden alone, talking.

"Forgive me for interrupting your privacy," I said, smiling at Neva, whose eyes told me by their glow what he had been saying to her, and what her reply had been.

"Lady Rowan, give us your blessing," said Liam in the tone of a triumphant lover. "Neva has promised to be my bride!"

"Of course she has," I said, "and I give you my blessing gladly, as will her father and your parents. But now there are grave matters to discuss."

"Yes," said Neva, sighing. "Liam will ride to Prayn to join his father tonight. I know it must be."

"I would escort King Verl's party to Verlain first, but I feel somehow that there is no time to be lost," said Liam.

"You are right. For Melyni's sake, at least," I said, and saw their startled expressions.

"For Melyni? What do you mean?" asked Liam. "To my mind, her total defeat is the best thing we can hope for."

"The defeat of her magic, yes," I said. "What do you say, Neva? Do you wish for her death?"

147

"I do not know," said Neva slowly, a troubled frown creasing her brow. "She has done much evil to me and others and yet – and yet – do not laugh at me for this – I cannot help pitying her."

"Pitying her! Why?" exclaimed Liam. "She would have killed you!"

"Yes, I know. She is possessed by darkness, by jealousy and pride and hatred, and so must also be very unhappy. I cannot help thinking so. Maybe I am foolish."

"You are not foolish," I said, putting my arm around her. "Your loving heart enables you to see more clearly than cold wisdom can see. Melyni is a victim of her heritage and her weaknesses, and she is indeed very unhappy. From her childhood she had a secret wish to be other than she is; to put aside her witch heritage and be respectable. Her mother, suspecting this, despised her and did not teach her all the dark arts."

"Let us thank the One for that!" said Liam. "She knows enough of them for my liking – too much."

"Yes. But had she had full control of her powers I would not have been able to escape her spells, nor would Neva have survived. There are many things she can do, but none are as deadly as she wishes."

"If she really did wish not to be a witch, why didn't she set aside her dark practices when her mother was destroyed?" asked Liam. "I know she pretended to do so. She swore allegiance to my father and let people think she was walking a straight path."

"Maybe she could not do it," said Neva.

"Could not. That is the answer," I said. "The dark castle was built with the blackest of magic, and evil dwells in its very stones. While she lived there, it would constantly call to her to use her witch nature, it would constantly work upon her faults – which are many. Her pride and vanity would grow. She was jealous of Neva's mother, and when King Verl fell into her hands (and this, I truly believe, was an accident, not a thing she had plotted) she saw that she could bind him to her by witchcraft. For she truly loves him, as much as she is capable of loving. I think she gave little thought to Neva, whom she considered a mere child, though she had hated Neva's mother, until she saw Neva's beauty, and heard her sing. Then the blackness of the witch nature took over: the jealousy, the pride, the old hatred of Queen Varena. And it possessed her."

"Yes," said Liam finally, "I see that. And I suppose I do pity her. And if there is any hope for her redemption I suppose I am willing to spare her. But I will never trust her."

"If – if you told her that I forgive her, Rowan," said Neva hesitantly, "would it help?"

"Someday it might," I said. "Who knows?"

"But what shall we do now, tonight?" asked Liam. "Shall I go to Prayn as I intended?"

"Yes. Neva, will you give him your stone and key to wear into battle, as a lady gives a knight her favor?"

"Of course," she said, surprised. She took the chain from around her neck and tied it to his sleeve.

"Tell your father that I am coming with reinforcements," I told him. "The People of the Wood are already on their way, but Neva

149

must free the captives in Melyni's secret room, and they will come with me."

So Liam went that evening, and the next morning the rest of us set out for Verlain. The dwarves, who could not bear to be parted from the princess so soon, came with us, riding their tough little mine ponies. Neva rode with her father and I walked at their side, for I can make good speed on foot. But I was troubled with a sense of urgency. We had no time to waste, I felt.

Someone else thought so, too, for we had hardly been on the journey for an hour when I felt a sudden surge of power, far greater than anything I could command. The forest shivered around us. The earth seemed to shift and the trees to melt. In less time than it took to describe this, it was over, and the entire party was murmuring and catching lost breaths and looking around in bewilderment.

"Look!" cried Thunel. "There is the pool where you and I first met, Princess! How can this be? We were miles away from it! What has happened?"

"This happened on my flight, too," said Neva, "only I was asleep and did not feel the change. I was sent from Rowan's wood into the deep forest."

"But who has power to do something like that?" King Verl asked dazedly. 'Rowan?"

"No, not I," I said. "Only the Lady of the Faerie has the power to change time and place. Evidently she wishes us to make haste. Let us be grateful and ask no questions."

The intervention of the Lady brought us to the gates of King Verl's palace before midday. Things there were in much confusion. Melyni, it seemed, was too busy to maintain her spells on the people at a distance. Some of them had fled, some were wandering about in a daze. Neva and I left the king to deal with them and went straight to the secret chamber. We found Melyni's maid Agathe there, but she fled at the sight of us, and we entered the chamber unhindered.

Without preamble, Neva began to sing the unspelling song. Thrice she sang it, and the room went mad. The mirror cracked, urns dissolved, tapestries and furniture disintegrated. In their place were the people of the wood and water, wind and rock, who had for decades been trapped. Even I was not prepared for their number. I was able to explain the situation without words, so it took only seconds. After thanking Neva for freeing them they all set out at once for Prayn. I paused only to kiss the princess and assure her that I would return as soon as possible. Then I, too, wrapped myself in wind, and departed.

The battle was at its height when we arrived, and was twofold: the High King, his magicians and wizards, and the Old Spirits from the wood fought with wand, staff and light against a host of shadow warriors; and the King's mortal men, led now by Prince Liam, fought the mortals who served Melyni. There were not many left. Maybe some had come out from under spells that held them and fled, others had been defeated. That part of the fight was under control. But, although the High King has great power and had vast force behind him, there was no end to the shadow army, for they were coming out of the very walls. They did not kill but froze and petrified and cast spells of madness. I could see at a glance that the King's army was tiring.

As the freed captives from Verlain rushed to join them I moved to Liam's side.

"Prince Liam, I have need of you," I said.

He is a worthy young man. Though the heat of battle was on him he did not hesitate or question but called to his comrade to take over and came with me.

"If I turn all my strength against the walls of Prayn I think I can destroy them," I said when we were away from the noise of the battle, "but I would destroy every living thing inside. It may be – I think it is likely -- that only Melyni remains but we cannot be sure and even if we were –"

"Yes," he said. "Neva forgave her and I agreed to try to save her. What can we do?"

"You have Neva's key. It will open doors at need, with or without a keyhole. You and I shall enter alone and bring her out."

"I am at your service, Lady Rowan," he said, and took the chain with the stone and key from his sleeve.

There was, at the far side of the outer wall, a small postern. No guards attacked when Liam held the key to the black wood and the door creaked open. We entered a dim and deserted courtyard and crossed it to the towering dark inner towers of Castle Prayn.

No one was within. We crossed the Great Hall and went up corridors and staircases, seeing no living being. Yet there was a restless whispering all around, and the shadows shifted and took ugly shapes, and a chill came from the walls. I saw the young prince shudder, but he went steadily forward.

She was in the top of the tower, where once her mirror had hung. I sensed her, and I knew that she also sensed me. It was well. While she concentrated on my coming she must loose her hold on the battle. When we reached the door at the top I knew she was on the other side, poised to act. I drew the wand I used only in great need. At my word the door shivered into dust.

Her spell hit the prince and bounced off, deflected by Neva's stone, barely missing Melyni as it returned. Before she could cast another I spoke.

I cannot tell you the word I used. It was from an old, old language and it named her family's true name, which they believed securely hidden. It froze her where she stood.

"It is over, Melyni," I said. "You have lost. You will come with us, and Prayn shall be destroyed."

She had no choice. I held her with the word, and she followed me. Prince Liam walked behind, his ring and Neva's stone upraised to keep off the evil whisperings of the wall. He has a quick understanding of the uses of powerful things; he will make a fine High King someday.

I asked Melyni if anyone else was in the castle.

"No," she said, the answer dragged from her reluctant lips. "I sent them all away."

It was what I had suspected. She had wished to use all the power of the castle for her army, and people inside its walls took some of its strength.

When we emerged from the main gates of the outer wall, we saw that the battle was over. The moment my word bound Melyni, the shadow army had stopped emerging, and with the help of Cassin and the others, those outside had been defeated. The few mortals left were captives.

The High King rode to meet us amid the cheering of his army of magicians. He dismounted and bowed low.

"Lady Rowan," he said, "I thank you. How good it is to see you back again! I was wondering if we could hold out until you arrived."

It is not finished yet," I said.

"Ah," said the King, turning his gaze on the walls of the Prayn. "Yes. We will make an end, once and for all."

He and I stood side by side, our wands touching at the ends to form a V, the tip of which pointed at the walls. Drawing on all our power we channeled it through the wands. To onlookers it was as if a great fountain of light burst from the V of our wands and flung itself against the walls. They shuddered and crashed and the light sprang over to the inner keep. It, too, fell. When we were done, nothing remained of Prayn but dust and ash, not even rubble.

When the cheering of the onlookers had died away we turned to Melyni. She stood very straight, her face white and her lips drawn in a tight line. Her eyes were fixed on me.

There was a silence as we regarded each other. Then she lifted her head and said coldly, "You have prevailed. Kill me and have done."

"Killing is not my way of solving problems, Melyni," I said.

"Nor mine," said the King. "It is messy and leaves untidy endings. What would it solve if we were to kill you? The darkness of your soul would linger in the ruins of your home, waiting to tempt the next comer to evil. Yet you deserve punishment for all that you have tried to do."

"Of course," she said, but her voice trembled slightly. "Imprisonment, then?"

"What say you, Lady Rowan?" asked the King. "It is your decision."

"I dislike keeping anyone imprisoned for any reason," I said. "This is my choice of punishment. In a year's time there will be a wedding. If you were to ask my friend Cassin, as you were wont to do, he would tell you that the bride is the fairest of them all – far more lovely than you could ever hope to be, for her beauty comes of a pure and loving heart. You shall attend that wedding, Melyni. And you shall give good wishes to the happy couple and dance the evening away."

She stared at me, her face going from white to crimson, then back to white. "Who is this bride?" she whispered.

"Princess Neva is the bride, and the groom is Prince Liam. Now do you perceive the extent of your punishment?"

She was silent for several moments. Then she gave a short little laugh. "It will be like dancing in red-hot slippers," she said. "Death would have been easier."

"How do you know?" the King asked. "You do not know what awaits you after death. And to see that you carry out this doom laid upon you by Lady Rowan, you shall come to my house and stay there until the wedding. You will not be able to escape,

155

though you will not be restrained by any physical means. You will serve my queen as one of her ladies in waiting."

"And after the wedding?" Melyni asked, licking her lips nervously.

"You will be free to stay or go, whatever you please. No one shall hinder you. Perhaps if you stay you might find meaning in life, and a better purpose than you have ever known."

There was a very long silence. Then, slowly, her proud head drooped and she spoke quietly. "Perhaps I may," she said.

And so it happened. Liam pleaded for an earlier wedding date at first, but finally bowed to the custom of a year-long betrothal. Besides, as King Verl pointed out, Neva was still very young, and he wanted her with him awhile longer. The year would go much too quickly, as it was, for him and those of us in Verlain who loved her.

And it did. I was with her often, for I still had things to teach her, but she spent much time with her father. King Verl would be a lonely man when she was gone.

The wedding took place in the great cathedral near the palace of the High King. It was a lovely but most unusual ceremony, for instead of the bride maidens who normally walked in the procession, there were seven dwarves, one of whom – who but Thunel? – held the bride's long train. She wore white and silver, and there was no doubt in anyone's mind, that day, that she was truly the fairest of them all, or that her voice was the sweetest ever heard.

After the ceremony, in the Great Hall, the guests went one by one to the draped dais to give their good wishes to the couple,

and among them was the one-time Princess of Prayn. She would have knelt before them, but Neva sprang up, raised her, kissed her, and thanked her for coming. The amazement on Melyni's face was worth seeing. And when she danced, she did not look as if her slippers were red hot. They were cooled by the dawning of a new and wholesome feeling, for their steps were beginning to take her in a new and wholesome direction. Thanks be to the One.

And so the prince and the snow singer lived happily ever after, with those they loved around them. May we all have such an ending to our own stories.

I bid you

Farewell

ABOUT THE AUTHOR

Florine De Veer was born in Calgary, Canada, and studied Library Arts at the Southern Alberta Institute of Technology. She worked for 25 twenty-five years as a bookseller, specializing in children's and young adult literature. She now lives in Charleston, South Carolina with her husband Clint, and their longtime housemate Eddie.

Made in the USA
San Bernardino, CA
27 November 2017